Praise for Mariann

"Marianne Martin is a wonderful sto[...] with a light, witty touch with language and a sensitivity to emotions of people in love. There is a tenderness and brightness to her characterizations that make the personalities quite beguiling." Ann Bannon

"*Under the Witness Tree* is a multi-dimensional love story woven with rich themes of family and the search for roots. This is a novel of discovery that reaches into the deeply personal and well beyond—into our community and its emerging history. Marianne Martin achieves new heights with this lovingly researched and intelligent novel." Katherine V. Forrest

"[*Under the Witness Tree*] was entertaining, and the way the pieces all came together was ultimately quite satisfying. Read it for the tight plot, for the mystery, for the romance, and don't miss this engaging story." *Midwest Book Review*

"Marianne Martin is a skilled writer who fully develops her characters and pulls the best from them. . . . *Under the Witness Tree* is a novel rich in character and storyline."
Mega Scene Book Review

"*Mirrors* is a very fine novel, well worth your time and treasure."
The Bay Area Reporter

"Not only does [*Love in the Balance*] have love and excitement, but it has issues very close to all of us."
The Alabama Forum Gaiety

"[*Legacy of Love*] is undoubtedly one of the finest . . . worth reading." *Our Own Community Press*

"[*Dawn of the Dance*] is a beautifully written love story, filled with gentleness and drama." *Mega Scene Book Review*

Also by Marianne K. Martin

Under the Witness Tree
Mirrors
Dawn of the Dance
Love in the Balance
Legacy of Love

NEVER ENDING

BY
MARIANNE K. MARTIN

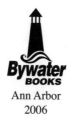

Bywater
BOOKS

Ann Arbor
2006

Bywater Books, Inc.
PO Box 3671
Ann Arbor MI 48106-3671

Printed in the United States of America on acid-free paper.

First Bywater Books Edition: February 2006

This book was first published by Naiad Press, Inc. in 1999.

Cover designer: Bonnie Liss (Phoenix Graphics)

ISBN 1-932859-14-4

For Jo

Acknowledgments

A very special thank you to Katherine for her friendship and much appreciated support.

My gratitude to Carol for her medical expertise in an area in which I have no experience; to Shannon and Eric for sharing the miracle of birth with me; and to Eric for being what I believe God intended a man to be.

My appreciation to Teressa and Julie for their proofreading time and input.

My thanks to Kate for the football game and for just being Kate.

A special thanks to Michele for a friendship full of much needed laughter.

And, a heartfelt thank you to my best friend and partner, Jo, for her love and loyalty.

Although based on many historical truths, this book is a work of fiction. The Clan of the Doe is used as a fictional symbol representing the challenges to survival that have been won and lost by many Native American clans.

Glossary

Eh-ho enna pon-o eth-o   Greek: *I have a pain here*

Gai'wiio'   Seneca: *Code of the Iroquois Prophet, Iroquois way of life*

ganodas'hago   Seneca: *storyteller's repertoire of tales*

go-ah'-wuk   Seneca: *daughter*

Hodinon'deoga'   Seneca: *Clan of the Doe*

hodinonhsonik   Seneca: *house-builders*

kä-yan-wän-deh'   Seneca: *niece*

neh, neh   Greek: *yes, yes*

Ögwe'o: weh   Seneca: *the Real People, the Original Beings*

orenda   Seneca: *spirit that connects one person to another and to an overall force*

Qua, my ne-wa-ah' na-o'-geh   Seneca: *Hail, my little deer*

sachem   Seneca: *tribal chief*

uc sote'   Seneca: *grandmother*

Prologue

No one could have known at the time how close the decision of a president, carried out by his generals, would come to annihilating an entire race.

When George Washington declared that the Iroquois should "not merely be overrun, but destroyed," the soil was burned barren of crops and longhouses. The streams ran red with the blood of women and children. But we know now that it didn't end there.

Hidden beneath the lifeless bodies of her mother and brother, Speaks With Eyes survived while General Sherman's men raped and killed and scalped. Years later, Mandra, Walks a Long Trail, buried three children claimed in death by measles, and bore a single heir at age forty-five. And during the assimilation, when Indian children were taken to white boarding schools and punished severely for speaking their native tongue, Juna, Little Bird, kept her language alive by speaking it only in her mind for six years. She returned to her family, not ashamed of them as expected, but determined that no child of hers would ever be taken from her and that each would be well versed in his or her heritage.

It was a strong line of Seneca matriarchs from which Sage Bristo descended, each one holding true to the traditions of the longhouse, each one overcoming the odds to preserve the *Gai'wiio'* and the language of the *Ogwe'o:weh*. NaNan Bristo had lost her daughter from the circle of the longhouse, but she had saved her granddaughter. And still it wasn't over.

Chapter 1

Sage paced anxiously the length of the modest Silverhorn living room, awaiting news she'd been dreading all week, while Ben finished a phone call. She paused at the picture of Sky Woman falling from the heavens, about to be caught on the back of a giant turtle—the creation of earth according to Iroquois tradition and one of the many stories Ben had told her as a child. It was the first picture Ben and Sarah had hung in their new home, and it had been in the same place on the wall since Sage could remember.

She hesitated at each of the front windows; the eyes that had watched the little reservation neighborhood change and grow over the years. She had always felt comfortable here, and welcomed. Even as her blood ties dwindled, her family here had grown. On the reservation, with these people, she found rejuvenation for her spirit. Her spirit lifted with the laughter in the children's eyes, grew wiser from the words of the old ones, and drew strength from the resilience of their hearts. Today, though, her spirit was sad. It was not good news she was about to hear.

She turned to look into the long familiar eyes of Ben Silverhorn. Seneca *sachem*, family confidante, he knew the history better than any other. He was himself a throwback to the days before disease and alcoholism and assimilation had taken from the Indian male his strength, his purpose, and his pride. In his voice she heard the pride that must have formed the speeches of Sagoyowatha, Red Jacket, the great Seneca orator. In the lines of his face, chiseled deep like carved cherry wood, she read the breadth of his humor and the depth of his heart. He was a silver-haired warrior fighting the battle for revival on a new battleground. Like NaNan Bristo, he was a traditionalist with a white man's education, trying to answer Thomas Paine's question in *Agrarian Justice*: Is it possible for civilized society to ever cure the poverty it has created?

"It comes down to you and Cimmie," he said, concern wrinkling the corners of his liquid brown eyes. "With Alma gone now, you are the last two women of childbearing age."

Sage Bristo ran her fingers through the short dark waves above her ear and turned her gaze to the window. "The cancer took her so fast. One day she was planning her marriage, three months later she was gone." She turned back to meet Ben's eyes. "It doesn't seem possible that it could be lost so easily, that after all the ones who went before have overcome . . . it could be gone in one lifetime."

"For the Clan of the Doe, yes. It would be over. Cimmie's

4

girls, when and if she has them, will have to carry the bloodline, and the heritage of the clan."

"Is this your not-so-subtle way of saying that you know I won't be the one bearing children?"

His laugh rumbled like novice air through a tuba, and Sage smiled in return. He was undoubtedly trying to picture the tall, toned figure of Sage Bristo so swollen at the belly that her long, sure stride was reduced to a long-legged waddle. It was enough to make anyone laugh, or cry.

In the days of her ancestors she would have been a *manly-hearted*, hunting game to feed her family and counting coups as a warrior to protect her clan. But a *manly-hearted* in today's society attuned her skills to become a winning athlete, a successful businesswoman, the family protector. And Sage was masterfully attuned.

"Stranger things have happened," he said in the midst of a broad smile, "but not in my lifetime."

"And if Cimmie were unable to have children, do you think I could let it end here?"

"Not as long as there was a single breath left in your lungs. You are the faithful seed of your *uc sote'*. But you should go home now. There's nothing more you can do here."

Chapter 2

The keys clicked rapidly in a flurry of motion from fingers racing to record a rush of thoughts, a chronicle of words, before their sequence was lost. They were flowing freely now, coming together nicely. The story of NaNan Bristo, in the words of Deanne Demore, was taking its first breaths of life. Hours of transposing tapes now gave forth a creative excitement that did not know exhaustion. Energy filled her and controlled her thoughts, and she never in all these years understood how.

What she did understand was the importance of giving the energy its full rein. Never plan on its appearance—never waste its presence. For days now Deanne had heeded that advice. She ate only when food was placed beside the computer, slept only when the energy waned. And, with a pad and pencil beside the bed, a full night of rest was rare. Her schedule was impossible to predict, and very difficult for anyone else to live around—especially a woman whose days and nights were as finely tuned as those of Sage Bristo. But Deanne was blessed with untethered time to write and with an understanding lover. She had but one concern: sending a woman of Sage's needs to bed too often alone.

Too wordy. Too wordy. Deanne hit the delete key and began again. She stopped mid-sentence to brush the fluffy gray tail from the keyboard for the third time. "You wanna *keep* that tail, Little Miss?" she warned, quickly finishing the sentence and rereading the paragraph.

A tall shadowed figure, arms folded across her chest, leaned a shoulder casually against the doorway. Unnoticed, Sage watched the woman with whom she'd shared the past four years, and marveled at how good it felt. Loving this woman, being loved by her, had given her more joy than she had ever known. Sage smiled as the ball of gray fur lying next to the keyboard rolled on her back at the sight of her and came precariously close to the edge. A belly of white fur popped into view while ash-gray legs stretched their mischievous white mittens into the air. With a playful flop the gray-and-white head dangled over the edge of the desk. Huge aqua-blue eyes blinked up at her in obvious affection.

"This silliness can mean only one thing," Deanne said, smiling as Sage's arms wrapped her shoulders from behind. "Who else do the girls do backflips over?"

Sage nuzzled Deanne's neck. "There's only one I want doing backflips tonight," she whispered, kissing the tender skin below her ear.

"Honey—"

"May I read it?"

"Well, actually my secretary here," she rubbed the kitten's soft belly, "just approved the rewrite. Although I don't know as I'd trust her judgment. Rub her belly and she'll tell you anything you want to hear." Sage's hand wandered gently over Deanne's breasts. "Don't even try it with her mother."

Sage relented with a kiss to her cheek and scrolled to the beginning of the chapter. She read silently over Deanne's shoulder.

> Wind Spirit graciously breathes her cool blessing through the window of the little reservation school. Her relief on a stifling hot summer day is scarcely noticed by children anxiously clearing their desks and scurrying to the door. Happy, laughing young Indians burst forth into the late afternoon sunshine and immediately forget the lessons of the day.
>
> NaNan Bristo, long licorice-dark hair lifting gently from her face on puffs of wind, watches from the window. Children's faces illuminated now in the sunlight, shining with carefree joy she knows will soon enough begin to show the effects of poverty. And after that, they will wear the mask of hopelessness. Yet, she accepts her challenge without question. She understands the magnitude of it. Its roots are sunk deep into a patriarchal society

bent on the destruction of all she holds sacred.

Still, she will teach her children the white man's math, teach them to speak and write their language, even to understand their culture, because it is necessary. But, also necessary are the lessons of the circle of harmony. Understanding their place in the circle of all life forms is each child's mission. NaNan Bristo's mission is to keep that thought alive.

"How am I going to thank you for this?" Sage stood and ran her fingers through Deanne's blonde streaked hair.

"For what, honey?"

"For everything I now see that it takes to write this book, a book that'll never even sell."

"I promised you a chronicle of your heritage. I know how important it is to you. Besides, what makes you think it won't sell?"

"You've got sex and violence being used against Indians in times of peace, love and spirituality, and the survival of an enemy two centuries old. Sort of crushes those guilt-free stereotypes. You really think white society's going to line up to buy it?" She looked down into Deanne's uplifted face. "What if all this work is just to write a legacy that'll be handed down to no one?"

"What's this about, honey, Alma's death?"

Sage changed her focus, let it skip over the desk and scan

9

the wall, then shook her head. "I've had this feeling for a long time. When she died I thought maybe it was about her. But it hasn't gone away."

"What feeling, Sage?"

When it was that she had begun to share such private thoughts she couldn't pinpoint. But it hadn't happened with any other lover, only Deanne. Something other than her love for Deanne had coaxed the thoughts and fears from their hidden caverns. She trusted her as she had trusted only her grandmother and sister before her. "I wish I had the luxury of dreams like NaNan. All I have is a sense of urgency. Like . . ."

Deanne waited patiently, eyes searching, trying to lock on to Sage's as they lifted away. She turned her chair to face Sage and took her hands.

Sage continued. "Like the feeling I had for weeks before I was attacked. Maybe it has to do with my own mortality."

Just the thought of Sage dying sent a March shiver through Deanne's body. "More likely it has to do with your concern for the survival of the clan. Besides"—she forced a playful frown through her discomfort—"you can't go anywhere. It's not on the schedule, and not even the Grim Reaper could get an unscheduled appointment out of Wendy."

Sage smiled and stroked Deanne's head. "That's probably it."

"That, and all your worrying over Cimmie conceiving. Things you have no control over. And when you don't have control you obsess."

"Thank you Dr. D. for that insightful and enlightening analysis."

"You'll pay a premium," she said with feigned seriousness. "My predictions, though, are free."

Sage raised her eyebrows. "Oh?"

"Uh-huh." She spread her hands and let them come to rest under the circumference of an imaginary crystal ball, and looked into her empty palms. "Cimmie is going to have a baby—a *girl* baby, and this book is going to be more important than you think."

"I wish I had your optimism."

Not optimism at all, only words she knew Sage needed to hear right now. She knew no other way to lighten her load. "You'll be telling the children of the Doe the stories yourself until you're 108 and haven't the breath for it anymore. And we'll let Grandma Bristo and the *Hodinon'deoga'* matriarchs before her do their own teaching through the book. We Anglos have a lot to learn from our dark-skinned sisters about the power of women. Knowledge that's been silenced far too long. I think you'll be surprised at the hunger it will feed."

Sage leaned down and kissed her tenderly. "And I'm hungry for you," she whispered.

Deanne returned the kiss just short of an excitement that would change her creative energy into something equally uncontrollable. "Before I send you off to bed alone, I want you to know that every part of me cries for your attention, except"—she furrowed her brow and pointed to the right side of her head—"this little creative lobe that has a schedule all of its own." She pressed the palm of Sage's hand to her lips. "Right now it's in overdrive, and I'm at its mercy. I'm sorry, honey."

"Never apologize for a gift," she said, kissing Deanne's head before turning to leave.

"Yes, ma'am." Deanne grinned. "Oh, and would you take Miss Fuzzy-butt here with you? I'm lucky the delete key is on the other side of the keyboard. As a secretary, she's a wash."

Chapter 3

"Afternoon, Wendy." Deanne peered through the doorway of Longhouse's assistant manager's office. "Sage around?"

In her characteristically brisk manner, Wendy Carnes tossed a quickly signed work order into the out-basket and looked up. "God, lady! Where have you been hiding? I haven't seen you in weeks." The phone rang, and with a raised index finger she indicated for Deanne to wait.

"Yes, Mr. Wells," she addressed, straightening her already erect posture and immediately accessing the correct paper on her full but efficiently arranged desk. "Order number 113786. We expected delivery this morning." She tilted her head, looking directly at Deanne but offering no expression. Her impatience was betrayed only by the point of her pen dotting ink marks on the corner of the invoice. "No, I'm afraid you don't understand," she began firmly. "If we do not receive shipment by tomorrow noon we will be placing the order with one of your competitors . . . noon. Good day, sir."

Deanne met her eyes with a grin. "Barracuda, thy name is Wendy."

"That's what I'm paid for. And if I *didn't* do it, you know who would . . . as she was signing my last paycheck. I'll bet we receive that order by ten AM."

"No bet here."

"Well, if he thinks our residents are going to suffer because of his inefficient ass, he needs a fiscal wake-up call . . . Now, Sage. I haven't seen her since nine. She disappears lately a couple of hours before lunch. She doesn't offer, I don't ask. All I can tell you is that she has a meeting scheduled in the conference room at two."

Deanne hustled swiftly through the center of Longhouse, with the doors of its modern apartments opening to center gardens flourishing beneath the giant glass atrium. She paid little notice to the greenery climbing the pillars and cascading over border rocks. Even the dazzle of rock-garden reds and purples, and chrysanthemum beds of sun-splashed yellow failed to attract her attention. She scanned the dining areas on the mezzanine and the tables tucked around the gardens for Sage's familiar lean against the back of a chair, the proud hold of her head. Not there.

Not that it was any sort of emergency that she see her right now. She just wanted to. It was easier now for her to recognize when time spent writing, the time away from Sage, began taking its toll. Even lack of sleep, she found, didn't have the effect that too little time with Sage had. There had never been anyone or anything else that so affected her life.

The kitchen was a bustle of activity. Leptka, with her Greek dramatics and broken English, herded her crew like too many capricious children, but no Sage.

"*Neh, neh.* She was here—stealing my baklava." Leptka waved her hand dismissively. "Under my nose . . . *Eh-ho enna pon-o eth-o*," she grumbled, grasping her forehead. The under-her-breath grumbling was likely not words of Greek humor, Deanne assumed. Yet the old woman's anger was unconvincing. With thick meaty fingers Leptka scooped up a generous serving of the coveted confection and plunked it into Deanne's hand. "You think she own the place."

Deanne smiled. "Thank you," she said, kissing the old woman on the cheek. Then, with a mouth full of baklava, she headed toward the barn.

The majestic old building, like the original farmhouse, had been beautifully restored. New wood stained a New England gray and a new roof gave the ancient fortress a fresh lease on life. The east end, sectioned and furnished with top-of-the-line equipment, now housed the maintenance department, vehicle repair facility, and the wood shop. The west end, with its hay loft still in use, was home for Niio and two other horses, as well as an elaborate tack room, and an eighteenth-century carriage belonging to one of the residents.

To Miss Anne's delight, Deanne's first tour of the grounds

was in that carriage. Of course, Miss Anne may not have been so pleased had she known what was included on that tour. Merely the remembrance made Deanne's heart quicken its pace—Sage at the rein, stopping often, but only long enough to tease Deanne's waiting lips, and laughing at her impatience with their slow pace through the populated areas. Then, finally arriving at the rock—a huge mass, emerging from the earth along the crest of the northwest bank of the lake. The most unusual rock Deanne had ever seen. And the feel of it, smooth as sculptured marble, warm with the afternoon sun. Its curved voluptuous mass, reminiscent of the heroic sensuality of a Rubens, cradled their bodies perfectly in her bosom.

"In her bosom she holds the secrets of the ages," Sage told her. "If you know how to read her language, she'll teach you the history of Mother Earth from the beginning of time." That day they had added another secret to the spirit of the rock. Just the thought of it sent a flush of heat over Deanne's body.

Without realizing it, Deanne had crossed the boulevard leading to the community's individual residences, passed by the drive to their home on the north shore, and found herself on the path winding along the northwest bank. On her way to the rock. On her way to Sage.

Some would call it psychic energy. Sage called it *orenda*, a spiritual energy. An Anglo with *orenda*. Who'd a thought! Certainly not Deanne, "Miss Practicality"—until four years ago. But now, whatever anyone cared to call it, Deanne knew it existed and had been with her a long time, manifesting itself since her college years in the form of dreams—guiding, directing, bringing her to Sage. Even when she had no idea what it meant. Even when she was sure her own logic knew better, the strength of the messages only increased. For the longest time the spirit had access to her only in her sleep. But NaNan Bristo was an incredible teacher, even now. Despite her stubbornness, Deanne learned to relax, to listen, to believe. And finally she would see it. When her mind gave up its anxiety and fear, she saw the truth pulling her like a lighthouse beacon through the fog. She saw not with her eyes, but with her heart.

The sight of her lover still stopped her breath short, still caused spontaneous sparks to ignite in the middle of her chest. From any distance. From just a look. Or from the way she moved, with the lightness of a cat and the haughty grace of an eagle. She hoped it would always be that way.

Deanne approached silently over the carpet of pine needles and moss, in an unspoken challenge to reach her unaware. Sage lay sleep-still on the rock, eyes closed to the hide-and-seek game the wind played with cotton-ball clouds. Deanne took two quiet steps closer while her eyes traveled the deep V of skin exposed where Sage's shirt lay open against her chest. Always the top two buttons undone.

"Come here," Sage said without opening her eyes. "Let me show you the secrets of the rock."

"Said the serpent to Eve."

"Nothing sinful about it," she smiled, pulling Deanne down on top of her.

"Mmm, only that you feel too good for it to be one-thirty in the afternoon," she returned, as Sage's long arms coiled around her back.

Sage touched Deanne's lips with a tender kiss. "Anything wrong?"

"No." She snuggled her face against Sage's neck. "I just miss you. How long will your meeting last?"

"Only about an hour. But Kasey and I are driving to Grand Rapids afterward to look for furniture for the conference room."

"It's going to be a late night." She began placing kisses the length of Sage's neck.

Sage nodded. "Kasey swears that if I can't find what I want there, it doesn't exist. I would have asked you to come, but I assumed you wouldn't afford yourself that much time away."

"It's not that I don't want to be with you. But I need to write while I can. The blocks will come soon enough."

Sage caressed the length of Deanne's back as the feel of her lover's body challenged the warmth of the sun. "Are you sure I can't tell you even one secret of the rock?"

"I'm afraid I won't let you stop at one, and you have a meeting, remember?"

Chapter 4

The Explorer maneuvered by rote along the left lane of I-96. Kasey dozed on and off in a half-reclined catnap through a series of business calls until the sudden silence of Sage's hypnotic voice woke her. She straightened into a stretch and slid the palms of her hands along the headliner as far back as she could reach. "What are you going to do if they outlaw using a phone while you're driving?"

"Won't happen." Sage's eyes remained on the road. "They already have one that's completely voice activated. How long have you and Connie been together now?"

Kasey turned and waited for eye contact from her friend, who she knew never asked anything without definite purpose, and when she got it replied, "Two-thousand, two-hundred and twenty-six days." She watched Sage shake her head and smile. "Why?"

"Do you really know how many days, or do you just throw out numbers to sound impressive?"

Kasey grinned. "I know."

"Ever thought about cheating on her?"

Kasey raised her eyebrows in mild surprise.

"Be honest," Sage added.

"Serious sit-down thought? No...What's going on?"

"Nothing." Almost inaudibly she muttered, "Literally." Her voice picked up again. "I'm just curious. I've never experienced a relationship like this before."

"Well, Del Martin I'm not. Six years hardly makes me an expert. But you know I'll be honest with you. What do you want to know?"

"What's normal?"

Kasey watched the deep brown eyes, focused intently ahead, and expected no other expression. "I anticipated a conversation something like this, sooner or later. I guess I kind of expected it to come from Deanne, though. This must be really bothering you."

The dark eyes, holding an expression too private to be read, came back, centered on her, then returned to the road without a word.

"It's normal for a couple's sex life to change. For them to make love less frequently. That *is* what you're asking, isn't it?"

"Partly."

"It's also normal to worry about what it means when it starts happening. Deanne is the one who has initiated the change, isn't she?"

"That surprises you—even after knowing me this long."

"Yes, I guess it does."

The Explorer eased back into the right lane, between a recycled winter-beater and a semi, to nose out the 28th Street exit. "I suppose I can't expect four years of a relationship to do much to alter a lifetime reputation, even in your eyes. I sense everyone is waiting for the inevitable other shoe."

Kasey laughed gently. "It was a reputation bigger than life, my friend. But I honestly haven't heard much in the way of rumors or speculation about your love life for some time now."

"They're there—every time I have dinner with my attorney or my assistant, or an attractive woman walks out of my office after an interview. Sharon keeps me informed"—Sage finally offered a slight smile—"even when I don't care to know."

"I hope she doesn't tell Deanne everything she hears."

Sage shook her head. "She knows better than that. She learned a hard lesson. But I employ a lot of lesbians. Deanne hears enough."

"Are you worried about her believing what she hears, or about her losing passion for you?"

"Maybe both."

"I worried every time Connie had a business lunch with a male client. Then I projected that worry into the bedroom— made incorrect assumptions about why we didn't make love. The truth is, it's just a natural progression of a relationship."

"Who says it's natural?"

"Relationship experts." Kasey acknowledged a subtle, but

unmistakable smirk on Sage's face. "Also, a lot of lesbian couples who've been together ten, fifteen, twenty years. They're finally starting to talk, and people are listening. You should read more."

"Huh, so I've been told."

"I told you once that love was the single most powerful emotion. I still believe that. Passion is nice—it's strong. But it's kind of like the tortoise and the hare. Love is what keeps the steady pace, growing almost unnoticed. Real love, enduring love, seeps deep into your soul, and like the deepest waters of the ocean, it's unaffected by the storms on the surface."

Sage was still looking straight ahead. She offered no comment, so Kasey continued. "That's the kind of love that keeps you around even when your lover is in an ugly mood. It keeps you in the same bed with her when she keeps you awake coughing all night and makes you want to hold her when she's sick and pull the hair off her face as she's throwing up in the toilet."

"Oh, thank you for *that* description."

"Sorry, but those are the times when you know."

"I do want that kind of love, but I want passion, too."

"So do I, and so do a bazillion other lesbians. It has helped for Connie and me to make special time each week so that we can be together undisturbed. Sometimes that effort alone brings back some of the earlier excitement of when we were first seeing each other. It's too easy to let daily routines or problems or work take top priority on your time."

"I respect Deanne's talent, and I love her more than

anything. But she's so unpredictable. She really *has* no routine or schedule." Sage raised her hand from the steering wheel in a motion of exasperation. "I never know where I fit."

"In her heart, Sage. She worships you."

Sage pulled into the busy parking lot without a word.

"I hope you're not thinking of looking elsewhere."

Sage turned to face her, eyes solidly on center. "I'd never leave Deanne."

"But if she ever knows you've cheated, Deanne will leave you."

Chapter 5

Jon Demore moved laboriously across a spacious living room, warm with the finely finished wood of treasured antique furniture, and greeted his daughter. "Isn't Sage coming?"

Deanne placed her hand in his thick-fingered and warm hand, and kissed his cheek. "She's going to try to get here before dinner."

"Auntie Dee!" squealed a three-foot-plus bundle of freckled energy, as she hurled herself magically from the doorway of the dining room into Deanne's arms.

"Aghhh," she groaned, straining to hold the wiggling weight that had wrapped both arms and legs around her. "You keep growing like this, you're going to knock me over next time." She turned her armful twice around and fell to the couch, then tickled her niece's sides until giggling made her release the bearlike grip. "How was your first plane ride?"

"It was cool! I got to sit by the window." Her eyes widened, and she pulled Deanne's head down to whisper in her ear. "Mom got sick in the bathroom of the plane. It went all over the mirror."

Deanne smiled, then whispered back, "Okay. I won't say anything."

"She's lying down on Grandma's bed."

"We'll let her rest until dinner. Where's your dad?"

"Putting the leaf in the table for Grandma."

"Dad, sit down and relax," sounded a familiar male voice. "Hey, Deeder, how's it going?"

Deanne kissed the freckled face before she rose. "Good," she said, crossing the room and hugging her younger brother. "The twins aren't with you?"

"Nah, twelve-year-olds think it's child abuse to have to go on vacation with their parents. Besides, we couldn't really afford it. They're staying with Chris's sister."

"Well, I'm glad you could come."

"Had to do it now if I was going to at all. The company's downsizing. I'll probably be the first to go. Chris's salary will have to be enough to get us through between jobs. It'll be a while before I get any vacation time built up again."

There was a soft knock at the door, and Sage let herself in. She greeted Deanne and her father with a smile and a bottle of Chardonnay, and was introduced to J.T. Demore for the first time.

"The way my parents talk, I expected you to walk through the door *without* opening it."

She matched him at eye-level, and returned a firm handshake. "They're fine people. They speak proudly of their children . . . and grandchildren." She made eye contact with large hazel-brown eyes peering out from under J.T.'s arm. "And who do we have here?"

"This is Jill, but she's better known as the Beaner," returned Deanne. "You wouldn't know she was this shy fifteen minutes ago."

The eyes disappeared quickly behind J.T., but returned to their curious scrutiny from a chosen spot on the couch, with Jill clamped to Deanne's arm.

The conversation was light and carried cordially through Jon's obvious pride in teaching Longhouse's master wood-working classes, then enthusiastically through plans to tour the Longhouse gardens. It continued around Mrs. Demore's inclusion and Chris Demore's introduction, and survived J.T.'s less-than-toasty reception. Yet conversation wasn't enough to keep from Deanne the fact that her brother and her lover were operating in an unmistakable field of polarity. Sage at one end—cool, polite, seemingly unaffected. J.T. at the other end—abrupt and detached. Deanne looked at her brother tucked into the corner of the love seat, arms folded across his chest. She watched his eyes survey the spacious room with its grand arched windows, and she knew what it was. His father, energized with ideas and plans, his mother stimulated and full of stories of her own, had been moved from near poverty into total comfort and a whole new kind of life because of one woman. The deduction was obvious. He was jealous of Sage, jealous of her ability to provide for his parents what he could not. She waited for Sage's eyes, held them momentarily, and realized that there was only so much she could do. This was something only they could work out, and it wouldn't be done in an afternoon.

The conversation lulled, and Jill stirred restlessly next to Deanne. Her eyes, however, remained fixed on Sage. Suddenly she started, "Are you really—"

"Jill Kay!" snapped J.T.

Sage looked from one to the other, eyes cool and expressionless.

"An Indian?" she finished, before ducking her head behind Deanne's arm.

Deanne released the breath that had stopped short of exhale and smiled. Not that their sexuality was a secret. They all knew in their hearts. But she saw no need for a discussion of it in open forum. Not today, anyway.

Sage leaned as far to her left as she could to catch a peek of one big hazel eye. "I am," she said. "Have you ever heard of the Iroquois Indians, or the Seneca tribe?"

Deanne moved her arm from in front of her niece and placed it around her waist so that Sage could see her shake her head.

"In Iroquois language the Seneca were called *hodinonhsonik*. That meant house-builders, because they built big long buildings called longhouses, where many families of a clan lived together. That's why I called this place Longhouse on the Lake."

27

"Do you have a horse?"

Sage smiled. "I do. Do you want to meet him?"

"Can I, Dad?"

"Maybe another time. We're gonna be eating soon."

"It'll be a good hour before we eat," his wife explained. "Let her go. It'll be fun for her."

"Take her on the nature trail," Deanne suggested.

"She doesn't need to go trampin' through the woods on a horse. She's never been on one before."

"There's really no need to worry," Sage reassured him. "It's safer than taking her to the mall." She studied his eyes, stubborn but resolute. A hero doesn't kick and scream; nor does a father if he is to remain one. "Remember," she added, "we walked these woods long before you. Why don't you come along?"

"Nah. Just be careful." He met the excited gleam in his daughter's eyes with the warning, "No broken bones or poison ivy."

"You know, not all Indians rode horses," Sage said, boosting a wide-eyed Jill onto Niio's massive back and swinging up behind her.

"Why not?"

"Some of them didn't need them. It depended on where they lived." They ambled slowly toward the nature trail, Jill giggling with excitement between Sage's arms. "My people hunted in woods like these and fished the lakes and streams. They grew crops in large gardens. There weren't any horses in their part of the country for a long time. The first Indians to ride horses lived in the wide open area out west."

"How did your people go places?"

"They walked or ran. Even the Indians out west did for a long, long time because at first there were no horses at all in America."

"How did they get here?"

"The Spanish brought them over from their country to Mexico on big sailing ships. Then eventually they came over the border into America." Sage caught a low hanging branch and lifted it away from their faces. "You know how scary Niio looked at first?" Jill nodded. "Think about how scary he'd be if you had never even seen a picture of a horse before. That's how they looked to the Indians at first. He's not so scary now, is he?"

Jill shook her head. "Let's make him run," she said, turning her head over her shoulder.

"Niio loves to run, but we have to let him be careful through here. While we're going slow, let's see how good your eyes are. Show me how many animals you can find before we get to the field."

Jill was quick to spot a pair of squirrels playing an acrobatic game of tag over high branches of oak and pine, and pointed out a crow the size of a laying hen watching them closely from its lofty perch. But she missed a small gray fox ducking into a thicket of dogwood, and her animated exclamations caused a flurry of motion that allowed her only a tail-end glimpse of a mother groundhog and her baby as they scampered into the brush.

Sage halted Niio near the edge of a clearing and sat very still. Jill turned her head, but before she could say a word, Sage spoke softly near her ear. "Stay very quiet. Tune your ears so you can hear messages whispered on the wind."

Jill held her breath, moving wide eyes from side to side without moving her head. A loud snort, deeper that that of a horse, sounded from the clearing. Sage put her finger to Jill's lips and nudged Niio forward to the edge of the path and stopped. In clear view now, and less than twenty feet away, were two spotted fawns no taller than Jill herself. They looked up from ankle-high grass but seemed unalarmed. One moved with long playful strides to a new spot, and both lowered their heads to continue grazing. "The mother will be close by," Sage whispered. "Listen for her to warn her babies."

Only seconds later, another snort that startled Jill echoed from the right. The fawns' heads snapped upward. Sage snugged her arms around Jill and whispered, "It's their mother. Look there."

Emerging from behind a rangy forsythia was a large doe. Her sensitive ears were turned in the direction of the huge beast waiting patiently for Sage's next command. She looked to her children plucking casual bites of wild grass between occasional glances her way, then back to the beast. She stepped forward, a graceful move that began with the stretch of her neck and undulated through her chest and down the length of her leg. Her eyes remained bravely fixed on the three creatures staring at her as she took two more steps toward them. Ears rotated at the movement of her fawns. Jill fidgeted in Sage's arms, and the doe quickened her steps, cutting the angle between potential danger and her babies. When she was directly in Niio's path she stopped, raised her head tall and stomped one front hoof loudly against the ground. The fawns raised their heads and, in the echo of their mother's warning, obediently bounded away. The doe held her position, turning only her ears to confirm their safe distance. When Niio lowered his head indifferently, she made her move. She whirled about and with only a few powerful steps, propelled herself into full stride across the field.

"Hurry, Sage," exclaimed Jill with all her penned up excitement. "Let's catch her!"

"They'd be tucked deep in the safest part of the woods by the time we got to the other side," she explained, giving Niio permission to enter the field. "Besides, why do you want to catch her?"

"So we can touch her."

"She would never let us. She's too afraid."

"She was coming right to us before Niio moved."

"Only to protect her babies. She would give up her life for them."

"But we wouldn't hurt them."

"No, but if we got them to trust us, she might trust other humans who would. We have to let her be just as she was born to be."

"Can we see them again?"

"We'll come back tomorrow. If we keep our distance and stay very quiet, we can watch them play. We have to enjoy them and learn from them without trying to change them." Sage placed the reins in Jill's hands. "Here. I'll teach you how to tell Niio where you want to go. Then we'll let him show you some really neat places."

Niio, with the patience of an angel-beast, walked and trotted and stopped and started. He carried them in circles, and eventually across the field. Then he showed Jill the secret places he had shared with Sage. They drank from a small pool of water, hidden in a cove of rocks, that was as clear as crystal and as cold as ice cream against the roof of her mouth. And when they were tired and sweaty, they rested deep in a hammock of oak and pine that stayed as cool as air-conditioning in midsummer.

"Sage?" Jill asked, as she ran the brush over what she could reach of Niio's belly. "Can I be an Indian?"

Sage smiled at the freckled innocence looking up at her. "Not by blood. You have to be born of parents who are Indian." The disappointment registered immediately in the big hazel eyes. "But," Sage continued, placing her hand over her heart, "in your heart you can be anything you want to be."

"I want to be like you."

"When I was about your age, I said that very same thing to my grandmother. She was very wise and knew many things. She told me, 'Every flower has its own beauty—every being has its own spirit. Look for what makes you special reflected in the eyes of others.' Do you know what she meant by that?"

Jill shook her head with a frown.

"She meant that it's okay to admire others, but you mustn't forget that you're special just the way you are."

Jill beamed with new-kitten gleam. "Auntie Dee, you have to call me by my new name—Ka-yan . . . wan . . ."

"Deh'," Sage finished.

With determined concentration, Jill repeated, *"Kä-yan-wän-deh'*. It means niece," she explained, so seriously that it made Deanne smile.

Deanne winked at Sage, then listened to a bubbling nonstop account of their ride all the way back to the house. Jill barely took a breath, then started the tale all over again the moment they walked in the door. How she would manage to talk *and* eat would be a wonder.

Deanne met Sage's eyes with a smile.

"Dispelling myths," Sage whispered, "one child at a time."

Chapter 6

The aroma of freshly brewed coffee, mixed with whisks of Observé L'Essence, cushioned the last cherished moments of early morning sleep. Deanne opened her eyes as Sage bent down to kiss her head. A silver woman, dancing at the end of a silver chain, fell from the gap of Sage's half-buttoned blouse and tickled her cheek.

Deanne smiled sleepily. "The scent of you could arouse me from death. Or, in this case, from a very erotic dream."

"Sorry. I tried not to wake you. You looked so peaceful."

Deanne slid her fingers down the opening of Sage's blouse until she reached a button, and unfastened it. "Did I have a smile on my face?"

"That good, huh?"

"One of the best of my recent recollections," she said, watching her own fingers as they opened another button.

Sage looked down at her open blouse and the fingers tracing their tips along the top of her bra. "Hold my place," she said, kissing Deanne's face before she stood. She picked up the phone on the nightstand and hit the speed dial. "Wendy, good morning. I need you to handle this morning's schedule in your usual efficient manner. I have an appointment at ten." She looked briefly at her watch before removing it and placing it on the nightstand. "Until then, I will be unavailable."

Deanne emerged from the bathroom as Sage draped the tailored lines of her beige slacks over the arm of the chair. "There are wonderful advantages to living with the boss," she said in a minty whisper. She slipped her arms around the proud, angular neck.

Sage closed her arms around the firm feel of Deanne's body. "So, tell me about this dream."

"Mmm." Deanne teased Sage's lips with tender touches of her own. "There was this tall, incredibly handsome woman"—her hands ventured beneath Sage's unbuttoned blouse and slipped it off her shoulders—"about your height, skin the color of creamed coffee, and ohhh so smooth." Deanne's lips traced the long neck muscle, while her fingers found the bra clasp. "But, her eyes"—she whispered as she lifted her head—"dark and deep, weren't nearly as alluring as yours."

Sage's hands, quickly losing their morning chill, began confirming the trim taper of Deanne's sides, the firm roundness of her buttocks. "Go on," she whispered into honey-gold hairs.

"She was doing wonderful things to my body . . . Mmm, yes like that . . . and her lips . . . came to mine . . ." as Sage's did, with passion controlled to a feather touch, brushing her lips and parting them to draw a breath that teased over the curve of her neck.

"Had she waited long for you—wanting you, aching for you?" Sage whispered against her throat.

Heat began to rise, creeping slowly, swallowing Deanne's body as it went. Her senses reached for the memory of the night, and before, to the ones that surely had inspired the dream.

Sage whispered again. "Did she take her time with you?"

"Oh yes." *Yes, so patient.* With her hands touching her as if for the first time—slow over the planes and hollows of her body. And with her lips, so warm and full, awakening as from a deep sleep each place they touched.

Sage's mouth began its possession of Deanne's, warm and wet, pressing and parting, then relented, leaving Deanne's lips waiting impatiently for their return. "Did she taste you?" Her mouth returned to tease, then relented again. "And tell you, when her mouth was hot against you, that she wanted only you?"

A soft surrendering sound escaped Deanne's throat. "I don't . . . I don't think so." The memory was becoming confused, beginning to melt with her body into the now. She was unable to discern between the velvet probe that during the night had traced its tip over her lips and sent pangs of desire to prick her everywhere, and the one that now stroked and circled her tongue and made her body ache.

Deanne was barely aware of her T-shirt having been

lifted and dropped to the floor, or of stripping off her own underwear and being joined on the bed.

What she was acutely aware of was the cool feel of the sheets against her naked skin, and the long silk of Sage's thigh sliding between her legs. *Yes, that was what was missing from the dream thoughts—the long press of her lover's body against her, and the smell of her, warm with response.*

Sage's hand began a long caress that started at Deanne's knee and traveled the length of her body. "Did she please you"—Sage felt Deanne's body shudder—"like this?"

She reversed the caress and lingered over the dips and hollows, and trailed long fingers through the edges of wetness until Deanne's body shuddered again.

"Or like this?" Sage whispered as her mouth began its journey, claiming the flesh of Deanne's neck and the tender depression at the bottom of her throat. Sage's lips continued their softness downward with increasing passion, arousing the sensitive skin of Deanne's breasts, commanding total surrender everywhere they touched.

Deanne's voice was husky and low. "That . . . yes, that." Her arms left their caressing along Sage's back and stretched across the coolness of the sheet. Her back arched, yielding, lifting exquisite softness to the full heat of Sage's mouth. Desire began its ascent, heat its descent.

"You please me," Deanne breathed heavily, "so well."

Sensations burst into brilliance. Pleasure flowed in waves that rushed and swelled and produced sounds that declared it far better than words.

Sage's mouth came again to Deanne's, letting her take it hungrily. Letting their kisses flare their passion, until Deanne's heartbeat pounded in her ears. Until her hands grasped Sage's hips and worked them into a feverish rhythm.

There was no existence for Deanne beyond the desire enveloping her. It was all-consuming, intensifying to a height she couldn't remember it ever having reached before. Deanne saw her beauty now defined in the dark sultriness of Sage's eyes, her breasts by the fervor of the hand cupping them. Her mouth existed only through the feel of Sage's lips upon it and her tongue within it.

She had no will, but that of the long, slow fingers stroking and stroking, and entering, and leaving, and stroking again. She had no want except to open completely to them, to push up for their entrance, to take the full length of the long silken strokes into her again and again.

Her senses soared helplessly out of her control and beyond all dreams, beyond all thoughts. Dipping in free fall, then caught by an updraft that sent them upward to breathtaking heights. Each time feeling she could go no higher, each time reaching the limit of her breath, until the final draft catapulted her into the weightlessness of orgasm.

Shooting all around her were showers of brilliance. And the brilliance was within, bursting from her, and the sound she heard was ecstasy hurling into space.

And then she was descending to earth in swirls of splendor. Horizons of sunset—oranges and fuchsias and pinks turning soft—swirling and blending and cooling to multitides of cerulean and sapphire and an ocean of teal.

Deanne held Sage tightly and floated on the heavy weight of the ocean, not wanting to open her eyes. Finally she whispered, "There's a very special place I want to take you."

Chapter 7

Deanne dialed the number she'd been tempted to call so many times. There were many reasons to justify it, only one that spoke against it. But it was a good one.

Hesitantly she asked, "Is this Lena Capra?"

"Yes."

"You don't know me, Mrs. Capra. My name is Deanne Demore. I'm in the process of writing a book entitled *The Women of the Doe*. It chronicles the—"

"I have nothing to do with that."

"But as the daughter of NaNan Bristo, you are an important link in the *Hodinon'deoga'* lineage."

"Who told you that?"

"I've been working with Ben Silverhorn . . . and Sage Bristo."

"Did she tell you to call me?"

"No, but—"

"I don't have anything to say to you."

The phone clicked dead.

Suddenly there was not a reason left holding enough strength to justify what she had just done. Only excuses. *If, but, because.* She could pick a word and begin any number of excuses for making that call. *If* Lena Capra had been receptive, it could have been the move that had finally opened communication between Sage and her mother. *But* just because this one didn't work, it didn't mean nothing would. *Because* as everyone knows the bond between mother and child, no matter how damaged, is worth saving. Yet towering above any of these excuses was the fact that she had deliberately defied Sage's will.

The weight of her defiance had lingered for days. Deanne watched Sage stare out over the balcony, the cup still only halfway to her lips. The glory of the sunset was reflected over the stillness of the lake, outlining silhouettes of stately pine in shades of pink and purple. But it wasn't that beauty Deanne saw in the dark recesses of Sage's eyes. It was something that lately refused her the enjoyment of things like sunsets and good dinners, and at times even her lover.

"Are you worried about Cimmie?" Deanne finally asked.

The dark eyes came back from their distance. The cup finished its trip to Sage's lips for an automatic sip, then Sage turned and looked directly into Deanne's eyes. "I have to go to New York tomorrow."

Deanne nodded. "I suspected as much."

"Can we postpone our vacation for a week?"

"As long as I don't find another rich, sexy woman who takes my breath away." Deanne smiled as she disappeared through the sliding glass door. Minutes later, she returned to lean against the railing in front of Sage. "Do you want me to go with you?"

"It wouldn't be much fun."

"That isn't why I would go."

Sage's eyes dropped to her cup. "Maybe next time."

"Hey," she said softly, leaning forward to draw her fingers through Sage's hair. "Don't shut me out. I'm family now, too. I know this has to be hard on Cimmie."

"Three years of trying, and some pimple-face can spend an hour in the back seat of a car and end up with a baby she doesn't even want." Sage shook her head.

"I know you're frustrated, honey. And the pressure Cimmie's feeling must be tremendous. Maybe there's something I can do to help. At least I can offer moral support."

"I'm not trying to shut you out, Deanne. There are some issues only Cimmie and I can decide on."

"Any of them have to do with your mother?"

"Her name is Lena. She's not my mother."

"Is that how Cimmie feels?"

"Cimmie still talks to her. But after she knew there was no genetic reason for her not conceiving, she should have stopped communications."

"It's part of her healing process."

"As long as she can work through her panic attacks, I don't see the necessity of keeping one of the causes of them in her life."

"Maybe she's trying to find a way to forgive her. This would be Lena's first grandchild."

"Yes, and she should not be allowed near it. Besides, the only heir of any importance to them would be a son by Jeremy."

Patience, thin as wet tissue, gave way quickly for Sage when the discussion involved her parents. Deanne tread lightly. "Isn't it possible that in her heart Lena doesn't share her husband's beliefs? That this is important to her even if it isn't to him? Maybe she doesn't know how to tell you."

"How important do you think an heir to the Doe could be to a woman who spent her life claiming an Italian heritage that never existed, a woman who denounced her own heritage, her own mother, for a man who isn't worthy of two seconds of my thought?" Sage took the last sip from her cup with an air that indicated that the discussion was over.

Yet Deanne pressed further than she knew she should. "You can't forgive her for that, can you?"

Sage's head snapped up abruptly. "No. I can't. For that—and for things you couldn't even conceive of." Her mind shuddered suddenly with a chilling awareness of isolation. She could feel the whoosh of a slamming closet door, clothes around her quaking to the wall, and a sense of dizzying blackness. Her world, for as long as it took—many times days—for her mother to unlock the door to her prison. Her throat tightened involuntarily, and she began fighting the tears of a little girl groping in the darkness for the jar she had hidden behind the shoeboxes. The secret that would

43

allow her to relieve herself when she couldn't hold her bladder any longer. A secret she guarded carefully, because soiling her clothes meant another severe beating. Through the narrow gap between the overhead shelf and the door, she felt the small slender hand find the edge of the blanket. Inch by inch the little girl worked the blanket through, resting her arms when they ached from working overhead. Finally, when the last of it was pulled through, she pushed the many pairs of shoes, with the smell of nyloned feet that still nauseated her to this day, to one side and padded the blanket into the corner as a cushion for her bruised body. She no longer needed the warnings whispered quickly as her mother passed the door. Her cries now stayed in her heart. Her thoughts struggled through the pain to follow the path she'd found that took her to her own private solace.

Sage closed her eyes with the little girl as she curled into a ball in the corner and listened for the words. Ancient words she knew by heart. "Sweet baby girl. You are the music that sings in my heart. You are the joy that lights my eyes." She uttered them all, each loving word her grandmother had spoken, over and over like an ancient chant wrapping their protective arms around her, their cadence masking the throbbing of her body. She whispered the words into the darkness, whispered them until they were proof enough that she was loved. Only then did the tears stop, and she could plot again the escape that would free her and Cimmie from the monster and his wife.

"It's eating at you, Sage," Deanne was saying, "just as it's probably eating at her. Not talking about it isn't healthy."

She watched her lover characteristically turn her head and tighten her jaw, a sign Deanne knew all too well. "Will you at least talk to Cimmie about it? You've got to find some way of forgiving her so that you can both start healing. Lena did what she did out of fear."

Sage picked up her cup and stood. "I learned only one thing from that woman—real love is what stands taller than fear."

Before Sage could leave the balcony, Deanne took her arm. "Wait . . . there's something that's been bothering me for days. I'm not sure how you're going to take this, but I have to tell you."

Sage looked into her eyes and waited.

"You wouldn't give me the information I needed for the book, and it really bothered me that it'll be incomplete. I called Lena and tried, unsuccessfully, to talk with her. I'm sorry. I did it even though I knew how you felt."

The chill from Sage's gaze froze Deanne's guilt instantly, before there was any chance of disguising it. There was no other admonishment. None was needed. Deanne knew where the line was, and she had crossed it.

"No," she said, "you don't know how I feel."

Chapter 8

Deanne sat staring at the luminous glare of the computer screen, but only Sage's face registered. She could still see it in her eyes—the look of disappointment, the once shining trust, tarnished.

How could she have been so presumptuous? To think that she, whose own mother wore her husband's worn-out work shoes so that Deanne could have new ones for school, could understand how it would feel to have your mother turn her back on you when all you needed was her arms around you. How could she possibly understand how Sage felt?

Her own cries in the night had been answered by a loving, gentle father who picked her up from her bad dream and carried her to the waiting arms of her mother. There her childhood fears were smothered against the old flannel nightgown, worn with age and smelling of laundry soap, and cradled in the soft billows of her mother's chest. Sleep came easily with her mother's soothing voice and the notes of a familiar lullaby.

She didn't understand Sage. She couldn't. Only Cimmie could understand. Only Cimmie could talk intelligently of resolution and healing—if there was to be any. It was clear. You cannot lead someone from the depths of the forest unless you've been there yourself. The best Deanne could offer was acceptance. And that, she was finding, was difficult enough.

Deanne scrolled through the pages she had written, looking for something that would help. What had gone wrong? How could a family, with a history of strengths capable of overcoming every manner of duress, produce a woman like Lena? She stopped at the beginning of the love story out of which Lena was born.

Bronze muscles glisten with perspiration, shirtless beneath the ebony shine of shoulder-length hair. NaNan watches, as she has for the last two weeks, as the strong young man works tirelessly to clear rocks from the construction site next to the school.

Each day she watches while the children eat their lunches, each night she dreams—of a quiet young warrior on a journey alone. The same young warrior who had visited her dreams years earlier, walking his journey without wisdom of medicine stories, but with a spirit cherished in the Iroquois man—pure and free of arrogance. He followed the river as it trickled over moss-covered rocks, quenching his thirst readily, seeking lessons of harmony.

This day, in the third week of her watching, he came to the door of the school. She had been waiting, expecting him as her dreams had foretold. For nights now the young warrior of her dream had followed the dry riverbed of sun-baked rocks.

"I wonder if I might drink from your well," he asked, passing an old cotton rag over his prominent brow. "I finished my water too early today."

She greeted him with ancient words he did not understand, and smiled.

"Your words are as beautiful as your smile, and I think almost as fascinating. I am Joseph Banks."

"You may quench your thirst at our well as often as you like, Joseph. And soon you will understand the language of the *Ögwe'o:weh*."

In the months to come NaNan taught him the language that had been nearly lost to his people, and told him the tales of the storyteller's *ganodas'hago*. He learned the traditions that the quiet years, the period of assimilation, had attempted to expunge. Traditions kept alive, secretly, faithfully, by the very women who had been stripped of their tribal powers. And while she spoke her lessons of harmony, he spoke to her the language of love.

The drums beat a union that produced one child. Lena Bristo was born of an educated traditional woman and a loving man who "came home every night with cash in his pocket and smelling of a hard day's work." Nothing in the first eight years of her life could lead anyone to suspect that Lena would eventually turn her back on her family and never come back.

Deanne searched further, scrolling through the sparse information that dealt with Lena's life, trying to find a theory that would settle her mind, even if she couldn't share it with Sage. She stopped scrolling to read. The love story was entering its final realm, a short six years later.

The sickness creeps through the reservation, taking not only the feeble and the very young. It takes teenagers and mothers and strong young men. Each day there is another death, until there is no escaping it.

With only the strength of his spirit, Joseph struggles through his fourth month to overcome the weakness that brings his body to its knees. Each day he works until the foreman sends him home. The cough racks his body each night until he spews blood and loses control of his water. But he refuses to leave his family to be admitted to the sanitarium. No one had ever returned from the white man's medicine.

NaNan kneels next to his bed on the day Joseph can no longer raise his body. Tears stain her brown cheeks.

His voice is a harsh whisper. "Do not shed tears for this useless body. It can serve you no longer. My spirit must be free of it—you must be free of it."

"You leave deep footprints, my husband, that neither wind nor water will wash away. I try to talk to my heart to make it understand, but it is in too much pain to listen."

"Promise me you will leave here and take our daughter where you will be safe . . . do whatever it takes."

With tear-blurred eyes she makes her promise as his eyes close for the last time. NaNan raises her head from the stillness of Joseph's chest to allow her spirit to soar with the freedom of his. "Soar now on the magic of eagle wings," she says aloud. "Leave the prison of pain and weakness, while my heart sheds tears that it will feel forever."

Chapter 9

"This isn't a discussion, Cim, it's an argument. And I don't care to continue it." Sage tossed the keys into the chair and crossed the living room of Cimmie's apartment without breaking stride.

Cimmie followed. "It is a discussion. You're just not comfortable about where it's going."

Sage continued toward the guest room without a word.

"Dammit, Sage. Don't walk away from me. I'm going to follow you until you talk this out." She entered the bedroom and stood determinedly as Sage began undressing. "What I'm trying to say is that regardless of how this child gets here, it has to be for the right reasons."

"And if you don't accept my eggs"—the long hands cut the air with a conductor's emphasis—"you'll have *no* child, but for all the right reasons? Somehow the logic of that eludes me."

"I can't have your child for your reasons—or Jeff's child for his reasons. Don't you understand?"

"No. Enlighten me."

Cimmie sat heavily on the edge of the bed and watched her sister gather toiletries from her bag. "Everything is black and white to you. This isn't at all black and white."

"This is about family, Cimmie, the only family I've ever known. That makes it clearly black and white." With an abrupt turn, she delivered her things to the bathroom and returned to whisk up her clothes.

"Sage, stop." Cimmie's voice softened with eye contact. "I know carrying on the heritage is important to you. And Jeff wants this baby so much I think he'd have it for me if he could. But for once I need someone to see this from my viewpoint." Sage had stopped, clothes in hand, and was listening. "Each time I fail I feel more like a lab experiment gone bad . . . or a worthless stock animal."

"Then stop doing this to yourself and use my eggs. It would be *your* child—yours and Jeff's. All I'm asking is that she be taught her heritage."

"Or he? And, what about Jeff and his feelings, and his family?"

"This is no surprise to him. He knew your heritage before he married you."

"But living it is a different matter, Sage. And we're asking a child to blend two cultures. I don't want any chance of conflict like what tore our family apart before we were even born."

"You're afraid of me, aren't you, Cim? Afraid I'll overstep

52

my bounds with Jeff." Her eyes clamped on to Cimmie's and forced them to falter. "There's only one way I can guarantee that that won't happen." She turned from Cimmie, disappeared into the bathroom and closed the door.

She couldn't say that the thought had never occurred to her. But it was long ago, merely a part of the youthful sorting that comes with maturity, a puff of wind, gone before serious contemplation. And why not? The assumption that Cimmie would bear children and that she would not was a natural one. Neither of them had ever doubted its validity.

As Sage brisked the towel over her body, she caught sight of herself in the long mirror behind the door. She stepped squarely in front of it and dropped the towel. Her hand stretched across the narrow span of abdomen between slightly protruding hipbones, not the defined washboard of her lover, but flat nonetheless. The thought wouldn't go away.

Would she really be able to face herself in the mirror with a belly stretched to the size of a basketball? Or envision herself a sitting Buddha, legs wide apart and an arm resting atop the encumbering protrusion, deep in a discussion of the pros and cons of breast-feeding? A pregnant woman?

She continued to stare into the mirror, trying to raise what proved to be too surrealistic a vision. A picture that should be beautiful, revered and celebrated for the uniqueness of its power. Instead, vanity, with its customary compliments and longing looks, stared obstinately back at her. Too vain, Sage Bristo? To give survival to the bloodline because of what it will do to your body? Even for nine months? Or is it an inability of your self-image to accommodate motherhood? Do your beliefs have the strength they need to alter a lifelong image? To fulfill your responsibility? Is it really a choice?

She smoothed the tail of her shirt, tailored to fit wrinkle-free under the waistband of her underwear, and fastened her jeans. Before Cimmie could ask, she passed the kitchen and offered simply, "I'm going out." Where personal problems, if they dare raise their ugly little heads, will be slapped with the hand of indifference. Where in their place will be music, played at a volume that virtually eliminates thought and stimulates primal movement.

Chapter 10

John Capra sat at his breakfast table on the open brick patio of his Long Island home, his attention centered on the pages of the *New York Times*. He was oblivious to his wife's numerous trips through the French doors to bring him fresh coffee and separate courses of breakfast so that nothing had to be reheated. He had made it clear years ago that reheated food wasn't worthy of human consumption. Neither was Lena's small talk worthy of his attention.

He overrode her sentence with his own. "Is Cimmie going to be able to give Jeff an heir? He comes from a fine Catholic family, that boy."

"I guess they're doing more tests. Jeff's tests were negative. There's no tubal blockage or asthenospermia," she explained. "Cimmie's cervical test and ultrasound were normal. Here, I wrote down the new ones—"

"Just a waste of time and money." He folded the newspaper precisely into its original folds and laid it next to his plate. Lena dutifully replaced his used cup with a fresh cup of coffee. He picked it up without acknowledgment. "They need to try a new round of fertility drugs. You told them I would pay for it, didn't you?"

"Yes, but Cimmie—"

"Jeff needs to assert himself as the head of the house and make these decisions," he said, rising to stand rod-straight above the table.

Lena's focus returned to her plate. Her response was barely audible. "They make decisions together. There are risks—"

"Everything's a risk," he said, leaving the table. "But a woman does what she has to."

Yes, a woman does what she must, she thought, returning to her now cold breakfast. What better testimony than her own life? How quickly she had learned the ways to acceptance from white society. Brown skin, if light enough, can be attributed to a more respected race. And Catholicism, with its huge congregations and active social calendars, offered a wide berth of social inclusion. You go to private schools, wear designer clothes, talk about the right things, and eventually you make the affiliations and meet the right man. The one with the job, the money, and the social position to give you the respectability you yearn for.

For the most part, she had done it all right. Hers had been the by-the-book life that others envied. The wife of a successful stockbroker could enjoy shopping on Fifth Avenue, dining regularly at the Tavern on the Green, and being included in almost any social circle. But more important, she could send her children to the best schools and give them everything needed to grow up accepted and respected by white society. They would never be embarrassed by ignorance or be associated with the uneducated, uncultured community of the reservation. Nor would they ever be taunted as heathens, or refused anything in life because of their birth blood. A good mother makes certain of those things, no matter what the sacrifice.

Her own mother never understood that importance. Merely leaving the decadence of the reservation and marrying a white man wasn't enough. NaNan Bristo never understood how wasteful the hours she made Lena spend sitting with her in the circle of harmony—surrounded by old women with fairy-tale visions of glory days clouding their eyes, and stubbornness crowding reason from their thoughts. They spoke ancient words that did nothing to change the hopelessness of their lives, and practiced useless rituals and chants that could do nothing to gain them jobs or respect in the white man's world. Practices that, as she grew older, became increasingly more embarrassing and difficult for Lena to hide from her peers.

Doctor Daniel, though, was the one who forced her to ride the fine line of emotion between love and hate. He was noble and good, hiring Indian medical assistants into his own practice, and helping those willing to help themselves. But she hated the uncounted hours her stepfather spent working the reservation clinic—for nothing. Not a penny, not even the satisfaction of knowing he had made a difference. He delivered babies no one could afford to raise and patched up alcoholics who found more than one way to kill themselves. She hated those efforts, not only because they took time away from her and were futile, but also because they were a senseless waste of his life. In the end, she was convinced; the reservation had taken him from her forever. The unending needs of a hopeless people had taxed his heart beyond its limits, and she could never forgive them, or him, for his death.

"Why don't you call Cimmie before she leaves for work," John was saying as Lena cleared the dishes to the kitchen. "Find out how the tests came out. You're her mother. You should know those things," he said, handing her the receiver and pushing the speaker button on the phone.

Chapter 11

"I hadn't imagined it would be this extraordinary." Deanne poised her camera atop the wooden porch railing of the little cottage as the morning sun glittered over the Atlantic water of Cape Cod Bay.

"I told you it was beautiful," Sage replied, joining her at the railing.

"Yes, but you prefaced it with 'Provincetown is the gay mecca of the east, lesbians wall-to-wall,' et cetera, et cetera."

"Which makes it *perfectly* beautiful." She watched Deanne turn her camera toward the Long Point Lighthouse and snap another frame. "I want this to be the best vacation you've ever had."

Deanne placed the camera on the deck chair and turned with a smile to stretch her arms around Sage's neck. "If last night is any indication, it will be." She pressed her lips to Sage's neck and moved them slowly down to the protruding collarbone. "What marvelous plans do you have for today?"

"Mmm, how about breakfast at the Portuguese Bakery, a little shopping . . ." She met Deanne's lips with a soft kiss. "And touch football with Kate Clinton?"

Deanne smiled approvingly. "Does she really play?"

"She puts on a pinney and gets right in there. Of course she plays the crowd as much as she plays the game. But she can throw a mean spiral."

Throughout the morning they canvassed the tiny shops of Commercial Street, gathering gifts for friends and buying T-shirts and sweatshirts for themselves. The narrow street became increasingly busy as last night's partiers ventured into the daylight, and the tour buses unloaded their seniors. By eleven-thirty the shops were packed, entertainers on every block were handing out flyers about their performances later that night, and the street had become one large sidewalk.

Sage took Deanne's hand as they wound through the crowd in front of Town Hall. Today Deanne didn't discreetly pull it away. Despite passing by a number of elderly heterosexual couples and couples with children resting on the benches that lined the sidewalk, she kept Sage's hand. Although she tried not to, she found herself looking at the faces they passed. A few sent glancing looks their way, but they were quick and expressionless. And there were no comments. Most took no notice at all.

It was a strange feeling, being suddenly the norm—the

favored, the accepted. As strange as a pauper on a prince's throne. It would take a little getting used to. But each day that she was here her mind became freer, with less and less thought wasted on what straights would or would not accept. Here, in this extraordinary place, it simply didn't matter what they thought. She squeezed Sage's hand and smiled. How wonderful it would be, she thought, to live every day of your life so free.

"Excuse me, excuse me," came a soft, husky voice from behind them. "Oh, honeys, I'm going to be so late." He squeezed around Deanne, all six-foot-two of him in his green satin short-shorts and platform shoes, and scurried toward the walkway leading to the Vixen.

Yet before he could exit the main sidewalk he was nearly knocked off his feet by an extended five-baby stroller, pushed aggressively onto the sidewalk by a woman totally oblivious to the havoc she was creating.

"Oh my god!" he squealed. "I've been hit by a goddamn bus!"

"Sorry," the woman said in a less-than-convincing tone.

Indignantly he rubbed the side of his leg. "If you're looking for the mouse with the big ears, sweetie, you made a wrong turn at the castle," he said, swinging the long strap to a little purse over his shoulder and hobbling away.

Before the woman could get her battering ram in motion again, Sage stepped in front of the stroller. "Excuse us," she said, pulling Deanne with her.

"Hence the 'Leave strollers outside' signs in front of the shops," noted Deanne.

"Exactly. Without those signs she'd push that bus right into these little shops and create all kinds of havoc. I've seen it happen."

Hand in hand, they made their way along the streets lined with cedar-shake sided cottages and houses, some with their doors so close to the sidewalk that it seemed opening them would bump a passing car. They paused here and there to admire a tiny yard with its miniature gardens and redbrick path and to take notice of small wooden plaques denoting houses that had been moved there by barge.

With plenty of time before the football game, they continued up the steep slope of Winslow Street to the Pilgrim Monument; then, up one hundred and sixteen steps and sixty ramps to its top.

The wind from the north forced their eyes nearly closed and glued their clothes to their bodies. It relented as they circled along the walkway toward the west and peered between bars and security fencing at a spectacular view of city and shore and Atlantic.

Sage slipped the leather backpack that she had carried all day off her shoulders and removed the heavy Hasselblad. "It's a shame these are so scratched up," she said, examining the Plexiglas view-ports. "And they don't open. You won't get any better pictures with this than you would a cheap little point-and-shoot."

"Watch me," Deanne replied, pulling the dark slide from the camera. She sat on the concrete floor and made herself as small as possible, ducking her head under the edge of a two-foot opening in the wall next to the floor. Carefully she slid the front of the camera between the bars.

"Be careful," Sage said, crouching down to grip the waistband of Deanne's pants.

"I couldn't slip between these bars if I tried. I just have to keep four-thousand dollars' worth of Hassey from taking a two-hundred-forty-foot dive."

She snapped frame after frame, moving from one opening to the next, recording the view and finishing with the stretch of shoreline wrapping Provincetown Harbor. How many ships, she wondered, had touched upon these shores? Their people leaving footprints on the land too deep for the tides to wash away.

Until now she hadn't considered Sage's thoughts. They stood together, looking out over the sun-gilded blues of the Atlantic and its coastline, wrinkled by the slender finger of land curling its come-here welcome to sea-weary travelers. What must she think of this marker? A monument erected to celebrate the beginning of a new life, a celebration of freedom from tyranny? Or a symbol of a new tyranny, the beginning of the end of life as her ancestors knew it?

"What are you thinking?" Deanne asked.

"How enduring the beauty of nature is. Try as it may, mankind hasn't destroyed that yet."

One hundred-plus lesbians packed the metal bleachers and sprawled along the sideline of the makeshift football field. They were there to see one of their favorite funny ladies up close and as personal as possible. And they wouldn't be disappointed.

Conspicuous in black shorts and pullover, and black-and-white cat-in-the-hat striped tights, Kate roamed the sidelines conversing and laughing and coaxing more women to play.

Sage and Deanne arrived in time to be waved on to the field. "My side, my side," Kate called. "Grab a pinney. Come on."

"Why are there so many on the other side?" Deanne asked, noticing the many smiling faces gathering on the other team.

Sage laughed and pulled a pinney over her head. "They're hoping we'll give the ball to Kate so that they have a legitimate reason to touch her below the waist."

The referee motioned for a representative from each team, said a few words to them, then chuckled her way back to the sideline. "I guess they're ready," she announced, "Names and all, so you can cheer on your favorite team. To your left," she pointed to the large huddle of women, "we have the Bushwhackers."

The crowd erupted into cheers and applause while the Bushwhackers held up their arms in acceptance. But the star they were there to watch quickly claimed the limelight. Kate ran to the sideline before the referee could announce her team, and started her own cheer.

"Give me a *C*," she shouted.

"*C*," the women shouted back.

"Give me an *L*."

"*L.*"

"Give me an *I*."

"*I.*"

"Give me a *T*."

"*T*," they shouted, beginning to laugh.

"Give me an *S*," Kate shouted with a big smile.

"*S.*"

"What's it spell?"

"*Clits!*"

She raised her arms to the laughing, cheering women, laughed with obvious mischief and turned to jog back to her team. "Don't hurt me now," she directed at the Bushwhackers. "I have a show to do at four."

With twenty-plus players on each team, the game consisted of a series of hopeful hail-Mary's, interrupted periodically with a short pass just over scrimmage or a suicidal attempt to run the ball.

After a halftime full of photo ops, the second half looked much like the first, except for Kate switching teams twice. It was getting late into the afternoon and still neither team had scored.

"Okay," Kate began, in the Clits's huddle once again, "who can throw the length of the field?"

"I can," Sage said.

"Good. Now someone run down there and catch the damn thing."

The ball was snapped, the count went to three, and Sage drifted behind the protection of the many bodies in the line while a soccer player with the legs of a cheetah raced down the field. As she cleared the clumps of players and neared the orange cone of the goal line, Sage launched a perfect spiral.

The players looked up and followed it in amazement into the arms of a receiver they hadn't expected to end up so far behind them. Touchdown Clits.

"Yeah!" Kate yelled with upstretched arms. She paraded among the players with high-fives and a Cheshire cat smile, making her way across the field. Near the bleachers she made an exaggerated look at her watch. "Oh," she said, looking up with a mischievous grin, "look what time it is. Gotta go."

Chapter 12

Downstairs Provincetown Shores was filled to capacity. Deanne was pleased that they had been able to get there early enough to get front row seats. Tonight was the one special thing that she was able to do for Sage. She'd made a few connections of her own during her interviewing years, and this one had turned into a special friendship.

"Michele was the first openly lesbian comedian to appear at the Comedy Club in Ann Arbor," Deanne was explaining while the six-foot-plus opening singer was lowering the microphone. "She gave me this really nice interview between shows. She talked with me right up until showtime. There were all these women waiting in the hallway outside her dressing room, and she opened the door to let me out first. As I turned to thank her, she was grinning and buttoning the buttons on her blouse, and said, 'Well that was fun.'"

Sage smiled. "I like her already."

"Please give it up now," the singer was saying, "for New York's Comic Queen, Michele Balan."

Looking very much like a petite version of Bette Midler, she approached the microphone, which was slowly drooping from its upright position. She pushed it up, and it immediately drooped again. She scanned the audience and quickly found the only heterosexual couple there.

"Does this look familiar to you?" she directed at the man. He laughed along with the women as Michele removed the microphone from its stand. "I was wondering," she said, holding it in front of the zipper of her jeans and bobbing it up and down. "It's been so long since I've seen one of these, I'd probably grab it and . . ." she brought it up, tapped it with her finger, and blew into the end of it. "Is this thing on?"

She waited for the laughter to quiet. "Do you like P-Town? It's great, isn't it? There's no place like it. Even at the beach you can tell you're in P-Town. If you're strolling along, and you hear show tunes blasting from every radio—you know you're on the men's beach." She chuckled with the audience and strolled the width of the stage. "Then when you start ducking Frisbees and footballs," she laughed and ducked an imaginary projectile, "you know you're on the dykes' side of the beach."

"I love P-Town, too. But they humiliate us so when we come here." She looked seriously at the first row. "They *do*. Yeah, you have all these comedians competing for the same audiences. So we have to resort to standing on the street corners and handing out flyers to get people to come to our show. What am I supposed to do—try to *look* funny? Tell a little sample joke?"

She laughed as she strutted back to the other end of the platform. "And it never fails. You know what someone always asks me?" The inside edges of her eyebrows nearly met as they pushed up into a questioning fold above her nose. "Are you funny?"

She shook her head and laughed and stopped her pacing at the center of the platform. "What do they expect me to say? No, I'm really not funny. Go home and read a book."

"Speaking of books," she continued after the laughter quieted, "there is a famous author, and good friend of mine here tonight."

"Nice segue," Sage said quietly as Michele pointed out a surprised Deanne in the front row.

"What time are you signing tomorrow?" she asked Deanne.

"Seven o'clock."

"Okay. Everyone come and join me at seven o'clock tomorrow night at Womencrafts. Deanne Demore will be signing her best-selling book *Real Women Wear Boots*. And I would tell you it's a good book even if I hadn't been curled up in front of a cozy fire in her living room when I read it."

"Thank you," Deanne offered, flushed and gracious. Then she leaned close to Sage's ear and whispered, "Why did she have to say I was famous?"

"Because you are," she whispered back. "They may not know your face when they see you walking down the street, but they know your name all over the country."

"This *is* the best vacation of my life," Deanne said, watching the harbor lights dance over ripples of black water. "I'm not going to want to go home."

From their table in the far corner of the Lobster Pot they enjoyed an unobstructed view of MacMillan Wharf, with the swaying masts of large sailboats and bobbing helms of the whale-watching boats barely silhouetted against a quickly darkening sky.

Her eyes remained fixed on the view as Deanne spoke. "Have you ever thought about how different you might have been if you had grown up in a world where your sexuality was the norm?"

"I don't think I've ever given it much thought," Sage replied, smiling to herself at the enjoyment she saw in her lover's face. "I never saw much point in dwelling on something that wasn't going to change."

"I've thought about it a lot," Deanne said, bringing a very blue-green gaze to rest on Sage. "I would have been much different. Much less afraid to express myself, more confident to try new things. Maybe more comfortable socially. But I wonder if I would have felt to need to write?"

"You mean that need would have been met in other ways?"

"Uh-huh. And I may have been less understanding of other people's pain."

"No. With parents like yours, you always would have been sensitive to that."

Deanne pondered and scanned again the postcard view of the harbor. "I wonder how things that *wouldn't* have occurred would have affected our lives"—her blue-green eyes returned to the candlelight—"arguments that never happened, secrets that never had to be kept, friendships lost or never gained?"

Or families lost? But it wouldn't have mattered, Sage thought. *Sexuality only made the tear wider.* "If it weren't sexual intolerance, it would be race or financial status, or"—Sage smiled slightly—"people who prefer cats to dogs."

Deanne returned the smile. "I suppose you're right. I guess that's why I don't want to leave this place."

"I can't think of any place I'd rather be than here—with the sound of Vivaldi, the taste of lobster," Sage said with the flickering of candlelight sparking her eyes, "and you."

No matter how many she'd heard, compliments from Sage still flowed as thick and sweet as fine sherry, and warmed her just as quickly. And Deanne knew how to get more. "In that order?" she asked, anticipating their intoxicating effects.

"Absolutely not . . . the sound of your voice against my ear touches me deeper than the finest strains of Vivaldi," she said, leaning intimately toward Deanne in their corner space. Her voice lowered to a tone more appropriately heard in the bedroom. "And the taste you leave on my lips is far sweeter than lobster."

Deanne could never pull her eyes from the magnetism of Sage's, even when she was aware that others were watching, even now when she knew Sage was about to kiss her in a public restaurant. She allowed Sage to take her flushed face in her hand and lean forward into a kiss. And the tenderness of her lips together with the effects of the wine allowed her to kiss her back. Sage was the one who pulled away before they crossed the line of respectability. A room full of people had disappeared during that moment. And to Deanne's surprise they were still there and paying no attention when she opened her eyes.

"Instead of taking the street back," Sage suggested, "let's walk the beach back."

Dark sand was being licked clean by the waves as they shushed all other sounds into the quiet of the night. Ahead the lights of the town, strung out like Christmas lights into the distance, defined the curve of the shoreline.

"Can you tell our light from here?" Deanne asked.

"No, but it's there. About a mile down. Are you going to be warm enough? There's more of a wind here than there is in town."

"Uh-huh." She pulled the hood of her jacket up and slid her arm around Sage's waist.

Sage lowered her arm from Deanne's shoulder and slid her fingers into the back pocket of Deanne's jeans.

"Why do you do that?"

"Because you have a nice butt," Sage replied. "Does it bother you?"

"No, I like it. I'm just glad you don't do it in public."

She looked at Deanne's hooded head resting against her shoulder. "Did I embarrass you at dinner?"

"No, I . . . " She lifted her head and gave Sage a kiss. "I wasn't at all embarrassed."

Sage smiled, teeth gleaming in the darkness. "Sharing this place with you has made this my best vacation too."

"It is incredible," she said, watching a night gull wading through the receding water just ahead. "I couldn't even capture this with my Hassey."

"You'll just have to experience it and enjoy it." She removed her hand from Deanne's pocket and wrapped her arm around her shoulder. "And remember it."

They walked in silence for a while, watching the waves rush to shore only inches from their stride, then creep back out for another run at their feet.

"I feel so lucky," Deanne began. "I was looking at this for a few minutes, imagining the look that would be in my mother's eyes if she were standing here. Remember how she looked when you showed her the gardens at Longhouse, and her face when she first saw the house?"

Sage nodded, then noticed Deanne wipe her face with the sleeve of her jacket. "Are you crying?" she asked, stopping to lift Deanne's face.

Tears glistened in the moonlight. "She was like a little girl. All full of wonder. She kept saying, 'I never thought I'd see anything like this.'" She wiped her face again. "And Dad. I don't think he knew what to say. You know, they've never been outside their hometown. They were born there, went to high school there, raised their family there. Mom was working and saving so that she could go to college when she got pregnant with Jeannie. I've never heard her say one word of regret. She just cleaned other people's houses so that I could go."

"Hey," Sage said softly, facing Deanne and pulling her into an embrace. "Let's bring them here—not during women's week. We could bring them in the spring, take them to Boston and Martha's Vineyard."

Deanne's face brightened. "Do you really think we could?"

"Your dad is doing so much better, and your mom is healthy. Why not?"

"I love you," she said with another kiss. "I could never do such nice things without you."

"Ah, so that's it."

"No," Deanne replied with a smile, "that's not it. And when we get a little bit farther down this beach I'll prove it to you."

Chapter 13

The sun splashed early morning brilliance over the glassy calm of the bay and glistened its fresh welcome over the drying sand of the beach. Sunlight sliced through the half-open vertical blinds and illuminated the room.

Breakfast hadn't been mentioned yet, but enough else had. Deanne sat stunned on the edge of the already made bed.

"You go from talking about whale-watching to having a baby? Is there a transition somewhere that I missed?" The surprise was evident in Deanne's voice. "How long have you been thinking about this?"

"I don't know," Sage replied seriously. "A while."

"You're not serious," stated Deanne. Although she could count the times on one hand that she knew Sage *not* to be serious. "You decided something this important without even discussing it with me?"

"We'll discuss it now."

Exasperated, Deanne sprang from the side of the bed. "No. You've made a decision without me, and now you're telling me about it." She had marched the length of the room and was starting back. "You've gone through whatever process it is you do in your mind and made this serious of a decision, a life-altering decision"—she threw her hand flippantly to the side—"just like you would make a business decision." Her stare was fixed on Sage sitting calmly in the chair next to the little table by the window. "This is what I get, isn't it? Because I like not having to make the plane reservations and to arrange for a rental car." She nodded her head to answer her own question. "I like not having to take the cars in for maintenance and not having to drive in unfamiliar places. I like that you are strong and confident and take charge. So this is what I get, isn't it?"

"I make decisions all the time, Deanne. It's just easier for me to do it."

"You're going to do this, aren't you? With or without my approval."

"I don't see that I have an option."

"No, of course you don't."

"I need your assurance that you'll raise this child if anything happens to me . . . make sure she knows where she came from."

"Oh, good. While you're at it, why don't you assume that I want to raise a child, then for emphasis"—her hands planted themselves firmly on her hips—"why don't you try to shake my soul with that nonsense about something happening to you?"

Sage's eyes never left Deanne's. Dark and cool, they seemed to absorb the shooting flames and cool them into harmless sparks. "You love children."

"I'm forty-seven."

"A very young forty-seven."

Deanne's eyes still crackled with anger. "Dammit, Sage." She pulled the heat of her gaze away to burn a hole through the little dinghy, floating inaccessibly at high tide, in the painting on the wall. "It doesn't matter what I say or what I think." Her eyes darted back to Sage's. "You already have a sperm donor and a date with a turkey baster, don't you?"

"I've talked with Ben."

Deanne turned her back, tilted her head toward the ceiling and closed her eyes.

"He's perfect," Sage said, rising to approach the abstinence of Deanne's back. "Good bloodline. Strong, healthy, intelligent. Raised by traditionalists to be a loving, nurturing man." She pressed her hands around the top of Deanne's arms and hesitated before drawing them slowly downward. "Who better to sire the next generation of the Doe?"

"This is not a business decision," she said tersely, even as the tension began to ease under the caressing of Sage's hands.

With an extended exhale, Deanne leaned back into Sage's embrace. "I've made you a part of every bit of my life. Am I ever going to be allowed to share yours?"

"You've been sharing my life for the past four years."

"Not as a partner, Sage." She turned and placed her hands against Sage's waist. "A true partner. What we've been doing is living together."

"As friends—and occasional lovers."

"I'm not any more satisfied with that than you are."

"Then change it."

Deanne stepped out of their embrace, but her focus remained on the inflexibility in Sage's eyes. "Oh no. I am *not* taking full responsibility for that. You want me to share your bed, but anything more intimate than what color to paint the bathroom or what to eat for dinner is too personal to share with me. Do you know how that makes me feel?"

Sage's eyes narrowed.

"No, of course you don't. Well, in case you're interested, it makes me feel like I'm just one overly long affair to you."

"You're not being fair. I've trusted you with things I've never told anyone else, even Cimmie."

"Sure, all those safe little snippets about life with NaNan. Oh yes and you have let me know you're human. You show passion during lovemaking, fear during a nightmare. Then there's that barely controlled anger at your parents. The emotions are all intact." She raised her eyebrows and shook her head. "You're human all right. What more could I ask?"

"Are you through?"

"I may as well be. God forbid I should have any effect on Sage Bristo's view of life, so meticulously set in stone, impermeable. A lot like your father, wouldn't you say?"

Sage's eyes darkened; her jaw muscles tightened into hard lines across her cheeks. "Don't ever say that again."

"I will say it again," she parried. "What if this baby's a boy? You going to destroy it and try again? Birth it and have Ben raise it?"

Sage pulled the black garment bag from the closet and quickly began shoving clothes into it.

Deanne was undaunted. "Are you willing to raise a boy when it won't carry the clan name? How much like John Capra are you?"

"This is obviously beyond your comprehension." She flipped the garment bag over her shoulder and scooped all but the keys to the rental car from the dresser. "Enjoy the rest of your vacation."

Chapter 14

"Cim. It's Dee. She's still not home."

There was a hesitation on the line, then Cimmie's voice, trying for a reassuring tone. "She hasn't shown up here yet. But that doesn't mean anything. She's not real pleased with me either right now. She needs time."

"Five days, Cim?" Deanne's voice quivered despite a conscious effort to steady it. "Do you think she's left me?"

"No, Deanne. I'm sure she—"

"But I said some pretty awful things. I was trying to hurt her."

"Listen—"

"I was furious to know that she shut me out like that. I lost control, Cimmie. I never should have compared her to her father. I've only driven her farther away."

"Deanne, stop and listen to me. Sage is strong willed and obstinate. But she's normally not impulsive. She's thinking this through somewhere."

"Where? In Tia's bed? Or some sexy thing I don't even know about?"

"Is that what you really think?"

"I don't know . . . sometimes. I lie here late at night and I can't get thoughts like that out of my mind. I think about all the times that I was too tired or too busy for her."

"This isn't about that."

"But what if it's enough justification? I was too busy mentally throwing dishes at her to realize what I may have done."

"Deanne, this is about feeling uprooted and abandoned, not about the state of your love life. I wish you could believe that."

Deanne finally slumped fully into the butter-soft leather of Sage's favorite chair. A leap of gray fur immediately claimed her lap. "I don't know what I believe. I only know what I fear."

"If we had been thinking like Sage, we would have foreseen this. Her sense of family is different from yours, or even mine. She recognizes only her Seneca heritage. Why do you think she goes to the reservation every month, like clockwork, like NaNan? The clan is her family, and it's dying. To her the decision was obvious."

"But she's not an island."

"In many ways she is. She trusts no one more than her-self. It's how she's survived without becoming a resentful, angry woman; and it's as remarkable as it is exasperating."

"I don't know how to handle this. What if she goes through with the insemination?"

"My therapist would say to go back to your bottom line and start there."

"What do you mean?"

"What is the most basic thing you do know?"

Practically unnoticed the kitten had crept up Deanne's chest and was pressing her wet nose against her chin. The loud purring could no doubt be heard through the phone. Deanne looked into the large aqua eyes and kissed the furry little face. "I love her."

"Enough to raise a child with her?"

"Yes."

"Then, I think we both have something we need to tell her."

Chapter 15

The ribbon of highway had straightened from the bows and cloverleafs of the city into an endless, colorless stretch. Misty-skirted mountains, dressed in their coats of many colors, waited for the morning sun to blink awake and rise above their frost-tinged ridges.

The nine-eleven, living up to its turbo-charged reputation, dropped effortlessly into fifth gear and flew past the rail posts lining the highway until they blended into a solid stripe.

Sage pressed the accelerator and welcomed the familiar surge of power. Eight-five. Ninety. Ninety-five. The Porsche hugged tightly to the road. Sage checked the rearview mirror, out over the whale tail. The road behind was as deserted as the miles ahead of her.

She pressed the pedal again, realizing how much she had missed the responsiveness, the speed. A hundred miles an hour. A hundred and five. Ten. The engine roared with its chance to blow out months of storage stiffness. It cruised comfortably at a hundred and fifteen.

Exhilaration filled Sage's head. She breathed deeply the air rushing through the vents. Mountain freshness mixed with the still new smell of the interior and the heat of the engine and swept cluttered thoughts from her mind.

There were no thoughts of destination, or destiny. There was nothing except the numbing vibration of the tires against the road, the wheel in her hands sensitive to her slightest movement. If only for a short time, she was in complete control, and it felt good.

She had driven for hours, unaware of the time until morning commuters invaded her raceway like herds of lumbering cattle. Her high-speed therapy slowed to an aggravating process of brake-and-change lane hopping. Why there wasn't some automatic roadway device that would eject vehicles trying to enter from an on-ramp at less than seventy miles an hour was beyond her. And there should be no one in the left lane without a car or a stomach capable of a hundred miles an hour.

Before long she had picked and woven her way out of the traffic and onto the past-beaten route to the reservation. Destination had sort of taken care of itself. Maybe destiny would as well.

Without the rush of speed and adrenaline to sweep them clear, thoughts began gathering again. They ignored her attempts to dismiss them. They stumbled over each other and crowded her mind with disorganization. Love bumping into promises. Self-image pushing at responsibility.

She hated clutter. Cleaning clutter was such damn hard work. Not allowing it in the first place was so much easier. *What good is an aspirin if you can't find it in the medicine cabinet?* Words of wisdom from NaNan's unwritten *Guide to Daily Living.* And yes, sometimes making it simple is difficult, but, she would promise, it pays in the long haul.

The road had turned to dirt. The Porsche navigated the ridges of the many ruts, reservoirs of yesterday's rain, and turned down a tread-worn lane between rows of grave markers.

Sage parked the car at the end, where a pile of cleared rocks was home for at least one inquisitive chipmunk that sat atop a flat blue-gray stone, chattering its questions and warnings in high-pitched squeaks, confident that it could dart down the closest crevice far quicker than such a large creature could move.

Sage knelt near the edge of the pile and picked up a fresh fallen maple wing. She peeled back the cover of the seed end and removed the green meat. Resting it on the ends of her fingers, she stretched out her offering. Patiently she waited through a series of nervous starts and stops before the chipmunk claimed it and scampered back to a safe distance to nibble its snack.

A short walk away, Sage knelt again. Scattered leaves, blown from a large sugar maple nearby, littered the small flower bed. She brushed them clear, and beneath was a stunning blanket of crimson dianthus, cobalt blue lobelia, and burgundy glow bugleweed. Favorites from her grand-mother's garden brought here to celebrate the freedom of their keeper's spirit. Sage plucked new shoots of wild grass from between the plants and pinched off the spent blossoms.

"They're thanking you, NaNan," she said aloud. "You tended them until they were healthy and strong; now they thank you with their beauty."

And how am I to thank you? For keeping me safe, and making me strong. For loving me. "By being selfish and prideful?" She stood out of frustration. All around her lay every reason for her to have a child. Old wooden markers, worn almost unintelligible by the elements, reminded her of hard-fought lives and unquestioned sacrifice. Mandra, Juna. Joseph Banks, lying next to the woman who carried his love in her heart until she died. Somehow they had all understood.

It wasn't until the moment, the second, she realized NaNan was dead that *she* began to understand. It began when she walked into the dark house that should have been warm with lamplight from the living room, that had instead the smell filling the air of a cake burned black in the oven. Fear immediately short-circuited all reason. She was weak, melting, empty, and frightened as she ran toward the kitchen. In the dining room her heart exploded in her chest. NaNan lay on the floor, her hand still gripping a handle on the bureau. But Sage didn't understand loss yet. She dropped to the floor, her mind in frantic search of a sign that her fear was wrong. Her hope shouted for warmth, for a blink, for breath, but her hands found only cold stillness. She searched quickly, desperately, for something that she could do, while her heart pounded disbelief. Blankets to warm her, blowing air into her lungs, massaging her heart. But the arm reaching the bureau was already stiff. Her grandmother was gone. And when the tears that accepted that began to flow, there began an understanding of what it meant to lose something irreplaceable.

Tears streamed down her face. Sage sat next to the flower bed, folded her arms over her knees, and lowered her head. For a long time she sat there, motionless. The grounds-keeper returned to his truck and delayed his mowing out of respect. He waited, while Sage weighed the sacrifice.

Aside from Deanne's reaction, and the possibility that she had lost her support, maybe even her love, there didn't seem to be much sacrifice to be made. Longhouse could be run from here, or anywhere she decided to stay, once her pregnancy became apparent. Or if she were willing to tolerate the indiscretions of Sharon and much of the gay community, she could stay home.

Sharon's response would be predictable and would echo the thoughts of many in the community less vocal than her. "Are you insane?" she would bark. "Butches don't get pregnant. Not on purpose anyway. A butch who ends up pregnant was either raped or way too slow getting their shit together."

How long ago was it that she felt the same way? When the lines that identified who she was, what she was about, were clear and obvious. And when had the lines become so hazy? Those that defined womanhood wandering and ignoring perimeters that had been set early and adhered to

87

faithfully. Were they no longer necessary? Only lines on a paper trying to confine spilled ink? And what of her role as a lesbian, with its lines always marked boldly in black magic marker? Where are they now? Maybe they had faded to make others more prominent, for one definition remained unmistakable—she was, and always would be, the go-ah'-wuk of the Doe.

Nine months of discomfort, some inconveniences, the pain of childbirth—she could tolerate it all. The possibility that she would have to do it without Deanne was what seemed unbearable. *Why that, NaNan? Why is it always the best thing that you have to give up?*

Even if Deanne gave in and stayed to raise a child with her, how soon would it be before unhappiness won out? Stress she didn't want, responsibility she didn't want. Disruptions to a way of life she had only begun to enjoy. How long would it take for the resentment to take its toll—one year? Three? And the child, bonded and vulnerable, would be risking the loss of a parent through no choice of her own.

It would be the biggest risk Sage had ever chosen to take. She was sure the sacrifice was more than she could stand to lose. Yet she had been granted a power so few are ever given. She alone had the power to save something from death. Because she had knelt there helplessly holding the one thing dearer to her than anything and felt the foreverness of death, she could not let it win this battle. Even if she knew it would be the last thing she did on this earth.

Chapter 16

Deanne hesitated at Sharon's door. She had waited as long as she dared. The cars lined the street; the basement was filled with people waiting for her. Why couldn't she have just called and told them she was violently ill? She was sick, sick to her heart. But, she couldn't do it. Thanks to Jon and Eleanor Demore, lying had never been a comfortable option. As uncomfortable as it was going to be, she was going to have to face them.

"Well, I see you've picked up at least one of Sage's bad habits—making a goddamn grand entrance," Sharon boomed at the bottom of the stairs. "I would've signed their books myself, but your picture's on the back cover."

"I'm sorry I'm late," she said, stepping into the gathering of women who had stopped their conversations to applaud her.

"For those of you who do not know her, this is author

Deanne Demore, or more commonly known around here as the prettier half of the reigning euchre champs."

Deanne made her way across the room to her seat of honor, at least temporarily relieved that the inevitable question hadn't yet been asked.

"I'll get you something to eat," offered Kasey. "Laura and Connie made meatballs and, of course, a ton of sweets."

"No, that's all right, Kase. I've kept everyone waiting long enough. Besides, I'm not hungry."

Kasey remained beside the chair as Deanne retrieved glasses and pen and notes from her briefcase. "Is everything okay, Deanne?"

"I'm fine," she said with a short glance into Kasey's eyes. "I just need to get started here."

"I'll get you a glass of water."

On her way to the kitchen, Kasey intercepted Sharon. "Don't," she said, turning Sharon by the arm and changing her direction.

"Don't what?"

"Ask the question I know you were about to ask of Deanne."

Kasey delivered the water, and then retreated to the back of the room to listen to her friend graciously answer questions. She watched her body language—erect, tight, precise. The Deanne of old, with worries clamped inside, using tonight to anesthetize some personal pain. She smiled with her lips, but not with her eyes. A sign Kasey had learned to recognize a long time ago and had hoped not to see again.

"How did you come up with the title?" someone asked.

"*Real Women Wear Boots* I think perfectly exemplifies the main character's work-boot logic. Jackie Madouse believes that black jeans can and should be worn everywhere, men should not be given positions of authority, and that Zena should quit screwin' around and ask Gabrielle to marry her." Deanne paused as the women cheered their agreement. "Uh-huh." She smiled. "I can see you're liking Jackie already. I suppose you want to know more about her now."

She acknowledged their expected response and continued. "Well, let's see. Jackie's favorite color is red, as in red truck, red leather jacket, and red lipstick on the women she dates. Her favorite movie is *Bound*, for obvious reasons. And her favorite food is steak, seared on both sides and grabbed off the grill before the blood stops flowing. But her most favorite thing is enjoying loud, sweaty sex in the back of her pickup on a hot summer night."

Deanne waited and smiled until the whistles and cheers quieted. Her timing was good tonight. The responses right on cue. At least something was working. She continued. "One of the things I like most about Jackie Madouse is her irreverence—like handling annoying lunchtime chatter from heterosexual coworkers by spending long minutes fashioning her ice cream into the shape of a vulva, then picking up the bowl and eating her creation with her tongue."

The response was immediate. Jackie was sold. Whatever

else she had to say, the laughing, cheering women were ready to hear it. Kasey grinned at the next question.

"So how much of you is there in Jackie Madouse?"

Sharon let go of a hearty laugh. "Yeah, we'd all like to know that. Myself, I'm trying to picture Sage in the back of a pickup."

"And you can keep on trying," Deanne said, and sipped from her water glass. "But to answer your question," she directed to the other woman, "Jackie Madouse dares to go where Deanne Demore never could. She has few inhibitions and even fewer fears. You know the times in your life when you wish you had reacted differently to a situation? Or had been able to say what you really thought? Or had come up with that very clever comeback? Well, Jackie did that for me."

"So would you say she's your alter ego?"

"If you change Webster's definition to 'another self' but *not* 'a double,' yes, I guess you can."

"Are you going to use Jackie in another book?"

"I think it's the only way I can shut her up." Deanne smiled and took another sip. "She has way too much to say."

Connie squeezed in behind Kasey and slipped her arms around her waist. "Deanne's so good at this," she whispered.

Kasey turned to reach Connie's ear. "There's something wrong."

With a frown, Connie studied their friend as she began signing books. "Sage?"

"When I'm helping Sharon clean up, why don't you see if she needs someone to talk to."

❖ ❖ ❖

The last of the women started up the stairs. Deanne tucked the zebrawood pen Sage had gotten her safely into its niche in her briefcase. She picked up her glass, but before she could rise, Connie sat down next to her.

"I know you're tired, Ms. Demore, but may I have your autograph?"

"Stop it," Deanne said with a smile.

"You did wonderfully tonight. You looked like you're actually becoming comfortable in the limelight."

"I think I'd still rather be asking the questions. And behind the camera is a whole lot easier. They wanted pictures with me."

"You can't hide the light of your star under a basket."

"Not with friends like you. I have to find a way to thank you all for hosting tonight for me."

"No thanks necessary. It wasn't difficult. Sharon knows every lesbian in the state of Michigan, which is wonderful when you *want* them to know something."

So intuitive of her friend. She knew. "Scary otherwise," Deanne returned.

"I'll help you carry this stuff to the car," she said, picking up the box next to the chair.

"If you feel like talking, you know it won't go any farther than Kasey." Connie stood by the driver's door and glanced in at Deanne.

"I don't," she answered, but made no attempt to start the

engine. Her head dropped back against the headrest; tears began rolling slowly down her cheeks.

"Oh, honey," Connie said, quickly moving around the front of the car and entering the passenger door. She pulled Deanne into an embrace and let her cry against her shoulder.

"That's right," Connie said softly. "Let it go."

"I don't know what to do . . . I don't know what to think."

Connie held her, not saying a word, letting her say it when she was ready, not chancing a wrong guess.

The tears kept coming. "She's been gone a week."

"It wasn't business this time?"

Deanne shook her head as she lifted it from Connie's shoulder. Then the words came spilling out, faster than the tears. And Connie listened, holding her hand, wiping tears from Deanne's cheeks, feeling the fears that had once been her own.

"I understand what you're feeling. Your stomach's a quivering mass, and you nibble on saltine crackers because it's all you can keep down. You lie awake at night going over every word, every expression until you finally cry yourself to sleep." She met Deanne's reddened eyes. "The thought that it could really be over sends a shock of fear through you that makes you feel like you're going to throw up, but there's nothing there to throw up. I do know how you feel."

"What did you do?"

"Finally? Just what you're doing now. I talked to a friend. It's important to know that you're not alone."

"You think I'm selfish, don't you?"

Connie shook her head. "I think you're frustrated and hurt."

"That doesn't give me the right to say what I did. It shouldn't matter if she wanted to have six kids, or give every last penny she had to the reservation and live in a shack. Love should be bigger than that." She looked into Connie's eyes, caring and unjudging. "It's the thing Sage wanted most in her life, what she thought she'd found in me." The tears began to flow once again. Deanne hung her head. "I've let her down. There's no reason for her to stay with me."

"Except that she loves you."

Eyes overflowing with tears looked up. "Then where is she?"

Connie squeezed Deanne's hand. "I'm going to stay with you tonight. I know you won't come to our house because you're afraid of not being there if she calls or comes home."

"I don't have the energy to argue with you."

"I know."

Chapter 17

The sound of a ball bouncing on concrete echoed off the west end of the little ranch-style house.

Phone calls from one end of the state to the other had proven futile. Efforts to locate Sage had come down to old-fashioned legwork. This second visit to Ben Silverhorn's sounded more promising. Jeff pushed his keys into the pocket of his Levi's and rounded the corner of the driveway toward the sounds.

"Do you know how hard it is to find someone when she doesn't want to be found?"

Sage turned at the sound of Jeff's voice. The ball careened off the backboard and bounced down the drive toward him. "If that were the case, you wouldn't have found me."

He picked up the basketball and dribbled his approach. "Cimmie and Deanne have been pretty concerned," he said, tossing up an awkward shot that hit the outside edge of the backboard.

"Must have left your white horse tied up out front." She retrieved the ball, turned and snapped the net with a long jumper.

"I'm here on my own. I thought you might want to talk about things."

"I don't."

He moved in quickly, scooped up the loose ball and dribbled to just outside the key. His shot bounced high off the edge of the rim. Sage waited while he chased it down and shot again. This one bounced up off the rim, then off the backboard, back to the rim, and finally dropped through the net. Before the ball touched the ground, Sage slapped it back to him. He shot again. She slapped it back.

They continued, Jeff moving from spot to spot to shoot, Sage retrieving, studying him as she would an opponent. He had the face of boyish innocence, and the build of a distance runner that promised to hold its own as long as the odds were even.

Finally he said, "Well, if we're not going to talk, we might as well play."

"You're warmed up and I'm tired. Even enough. Name your game."

"Make it-take it. To ten," he said, handing her the ball.

"Only if you don't want to shoot this game," she returned, dropping the ball back in front of him.

Jeff picked up the ball, then stared for a long second into the cool brown eyes that studied him. There may have been an almost undetectable glint of excitement at the challenge, but he wasn't sure. He pulled the ball into a protective crouch, made a weak head and shoulder fake to his left and started to drive right.

Sage tapped the ball out of his dribble. He scrambled after it and started back in. Sage closed the distance quickly before he was within shooting range, overplayed his right and forced him to go left. His control was bad, and she tapped it away again. This time after he recovered it he put his shoulder down and drove right into her. Sage held her ground. He stopped and tried to force a shot over her, but she blocked it. In frustration, he reclaimed the loose ball from behind him and quickly sent a long air ball in the direction of the basket.

Sage claimed the ball and with three long strides was behind the chalked free-throw line. She pivoted immediately into a jump shot that sent her first point through the hoop.

Jeff brought the ball back to what he thought was good defensive distance and handed her the ball. Her foot fake caused him to lean left, and she pushed up into another jumper for her second point. He returned the ball again only to be faked right as Sage drove to the left and an easy lay-up.

His defense was ineffective. He played too tight, she drove around him—too loose, and she shot over him. Before he could catch his breath, she had eight points, and he was bumping and pushing her drive to nine like a street kid.

"Game point," she said, dribbling casually to her right and protecting the ball with her body. She stopped halfway down the right side of the key and hooked the ball high and soft over her head for number ten.

Jeff gathered in the ball and shook his head. Sage pulled the bottom of her T-shirt up to wipe the sweat from her face and started toward the edge of the driveway.

"Two out of three," he called.

Sage stopped and turned. "What, you suddenly remembered how to do a jump shot?"

His smile crinkled into lines around his eyes. It was an honest smile. "Straight one-on-one. Fouls and free throws."

"You're a masochist."

He grinned. "But I'll bet you're enjoying it."

"Scary thought. So would a dominatrix." She tapped the ball as he held it, indicating that she was ready. "At least take a three-spot."

"Three-zip," he grinned, with a grasp on reality.

He was just short of her height, with long arms and a spring of a jump. But, like a lot of men, he had natural physical ability and no technical skills. He jerked instead of glided, pushed instead of rolled. Threw up bricks because he shot with only his arm and not his wrist.

Over and over he came at her, only to have the ball tapped away or stolen, his shots rushed or blocked. But he didn't give up. While Sage faked, drove, and jumped her way to point after point, he hustled to correct his position, fought her for every rebound, and called his fouls honestly.

At 3-9, Jeff tried a foot fake left and started to drive right.

"No," Sage said, tapping the ball, but not hard enough to make him lose it. "Your dribble's wide open." She tapped it again. "Protect it with your body."

He tried to adjust. She pushed his arm down.

"No, not with your arm—your body. Bring the dribble back behind your front leg." She slapped his left thigh. He adjusted again.

"Good. Now keep it low . . . Go," she directed. "Drive."

He continued toward the basket. Shoulder to chest with Sage, he pushed off into a lay-up, muscled the ball past Sage's hand, but missed the shot.

"My foul," she said, handing him the ball.

"Incidental contact. I just missed it."

"I had your shoulder all the way up. Now take the foul shot."

He shrugged, set his feet behind the chalk, bounced the ball twice, and this time pushed the ball through the hoop.

"Four-nine," she said, an arm's distance away. "Give yourself room this time. Get too close and you cut down your options."

He took a second to think, then brought the ball up to shoot. Sage closed in with one step and blocked the ball before it left his hands.

"No fake is even worse than a weak one unless you have a good jump shot." She gave him arm's distance again. "Convince me. If I step or lean, bring it up and shoot. If I don't, drive."

The lesson computed immediately. Jeff faked left. Sage held her ground, eyes focused on his hips. He put the ball down and in a quick step, drove left. Sage moved defensively a step behind but caught up when he nearly lost control of his dribble. He stopped his drive and opted for an off-balance shot that bounced off the rim.

"If you had a left hand, you would've had me beat," Sage remarked, collecting the rebound.

She was behind the line in two steps, with Jeff hustling into defensive position. She convinced him with a step and a dribble right, then sent the ball between her legs to the left, and drove to an easy left-hand lay-up.

"I should have challenged you to pig," he laughed.

"And miss all this fun?" she returned, snapping a hard pass toward his chest.

"Or getting to know you?"

Sage sent him a skeptical frown.

"I've learned more about you in less than an hour than I have in the past four years."

"Vital, national headline information, I'm sure." She added a half-turned smile and offered him her water bottle as she dropped onto the grass.

Jeff tipped his head back and squeezed a long swallow from the bottle before handing it back, then made a seat of the basketball. "Men don't usually talk about things like virtue and integrity. They play basketball or touch football. They don't even talk about teamwork. They just do it."

"So do some women."

For a minute neither of them spoke, then Jeff began again. "But I do enjoy discussions about more important issues than the Yankees chances for the World Series . . . Cimmie and I have good conversations. We can talk about anything."

"Has anyone ever told you that you're a strange man, Jeff?"

He smiled and chuckled softly. "Actually, I think that's my sex appeal."

Sage finally smiled a full smile. "She's not after your body, huh?"

"Well, until we started trying to make babies, I almost forgot what it was like." Aware of her silence, he added, "Probably things you'd rather not know."

"No, it's okay. I'm relating."

"But you know? I've never felt more loved or appreciated by anyone."

"Still relating."

They traded squirts from the water bottle, undisturbed by a long interlude of silence. Sage lay back on the grass and tucked her hands behind her head as a pillow. Jeff watched a killdeer, squawking and dragging what appeared to be a broken wing across the middle of the yard, as a stray mutt crossed the back near the fence. As soon as the threat was gone, the bird pulled in her wing and scurried back to sit on her nest.

This time Sage spoke to break the silence. "Ever felt the weight of a life-and-death situation? And you knew you could save it, but you might lose yourself doing it?"

"Not until now."

She raised her head to look directly at him.

"I never had to understand what extinction meant until now . . . The finality of a last breath, the end of a species—or even a family."

Sage relaxed her head again and closed her eyes. She wanted only to hear the words, and allow them her full and complete attention. Was it possible that someone like him really understood? A non-Indian, a non-Jew? An Anglo?

"I've never had to understand it," he continued. "The branches of my family tree could be mistaken for a small forest. And there's no end in sight. The closest I came to understanding was buying endangered species stamps."

"And not a brown face among them." Sage sat up and draped her arms over her knees. "I learned very young not to believe in the altruism of mankind. Changing our lot in life is our own responsibility. And we had damn well better take every opportunity there is to do it. Sometimes, though, I feel as if I'm standing on a slick riverbank, stretching my hand to someone swirling in an undertow."

Jeff let her words carry across the yard without any of his own to muffle their intensity. If there had been any doubt in his mind, it was gone. Of course she would bear a child. She would bear as many as it took. It was as personal to her as raising a child was to him. And it wasn't out of selfishness.

"I know Cimmie wanted to tell you this," he began, "but I realize now that it's important that I be the one to tell you. As well as Cimmie knows me, knows how I believe, she still feared that the reactions of your parents would repeat themselves in our life. I think I've finally convinced her that it won't happen. There have been times that I felt I wanted children more than she did. But it was just her fears, and there are layers of them." He looked into Sage's attentive eyes and realized how many she herself must have overcome. "We've been busy peeling off layers, and we're not home free. But if you're still offering your eggs, we're accepting."

For a moment Sage was reluctant to believe what she was hearing. She had resolved herself to her mission, resolved herself to fulfilling it alone. Did she dare think any differently now?

"Do you realize what this would involve?"

"I realize that we'd be making a family together," he replied, "all of us, including Deanne."

"And nothing about that worries you?"

He was leaning forward on his knees, watching Sage peel grass blades in half. "A lot worries me. Bringing a healthy baby into the world, making good decisions, being a good parent." He cocked his head to the side and met Sage's eyes. "I'm not worried about you."

"That makes you the only one who isn't."

"Kind of ironic, isn't it?"

Sage nodded. "Even though you know how important having a girl is to me?"

"This is going to surprise you, but I'd rather have a girl."

"Why?"

"I worry about raising a boy. I would raise my son to be loving and caring. No son of mine would swing cats by their tails or expose himself to passing motorists on a dare. He would not sleep with a girl for kudos from friends and then disrespect her. How hard do you think it would be for a boy like that to survive today without being bullied and harassed? What kind of hell would he have to go through to stay true to his values?"

"The same hell you must have gone through."

He shrugged his shoulders. "No, much worse today."

Sage watched him closely, looking for signs of insincerity—a nervous tick, eyes shifting away from hers. But he was steady, solid. "Are you sure there's no ancient Seneca blood running through your veins?"

He smiled as he stood and offered her a hand up. "Come on, Chief. Let's go home."

Chapter 18

If she could have handled more than orange juice and an English muffin, brunch would have been a nice idea. As it turned out, it was the only way she could get Connie to give up the notion that she needed to stay all day Sunday as well. Without a promise that Deanne would call her tonight, she would have sent Kasey home alone again.

Deanne pulled up the winding drive, strangely relieved to be coming home alone. The beautiful two-story structure, with its brick of taupes and tans and warm wood trim, hugged the sloping shore of the lake. Secluded and tranquil, the peaks and valleys of its roof nestled against the backdrop of giant white pine. Home. At least it had been until a week ago.

Sage said it herself, the day she first showed Deanne the beauty of the lake. Pointing out where the house would be built, she told her, "An expensive house isn't necessarily a home. To be that, it has to be shared in love." And it had been. But unless it was again, Deanne would leave it. And Sage. As beautiful as it was here, and as sure as she was that she would not be able to live in such luxury again, she would never again compromise love for security. Never.

The one thing she didn't worry about was the welfare of her parents. Regardless of the state of her relationship with their daughter, Sage would do nothing to disrupt their lives. Of that Deanne was sure. She knew, too, that although she would work as many jobs as necessary to pay Sage back, the money would be deposited in her parents' bank account.

She had thought it through carefully, looking at every possible scenario, even when at times her emotions made her question the rationality of any decision. She had to be prepared. If Sage were to call and tell her it was over, the decision to take only her clothes and her books and her kitten would already be made. If Sage found reason enough to tell her she'd been sleeping with someone else, Deanne Demore would not be made a fool of. The ultimatum would be given. She would only stay if Sage asked for forgiveness and promised her it would never happen again. Even then, she may never again be able to completely trust her.

But if Sage couldn't make that promise, it would be over. *I'll be no fool this time—not for money, or what it can buy, not for passion and the heat of the best sex I've ever had . . . not for the pretense of love.*

And if Sage offered nothing, no explanation beyond that she had needed time to think, would anything have changed?

It had taken her all week to come back to that strength, to

make her way through the fears, and the anger that at first had been directed at Sage, then more appropriately at herself. The years with Sage had made her emotionally soft, vulnerable to the worse kind of pain. It took concentrated effort to regain control and bolster her defenses. The demons weren't gone, but she had opened the door to the darkness and forced herself to look each demon in the face. One at a time they were no bigger than the strength it took to submit her first manuscript.

Yet, all the bolstering in the world didn't seem capable of easing the one possibility she feared most: that Sage no longer wanted *her* under any condition.

The key turned too easily in the lock. Before she could stop it, hope raced past the thought that she just may have forgotten to lock the door and filled her with excitement. *Sage.*

Deanne dropped her things on the bench in the foyer, rushed past the dining room and the library and through the living room, hurriedly searching for signs that Sage was home. "Please," she whispered prayerfully, "please be here."

Deanne's eyes watered immediately at the sight of her, hands braced against the balcony railing, looking out over the lake. She approached through the open door, wrapped her arms around Sage's waist and buried her face against the crisp white shirt. The tears began naturally, quietly. There would be no questions. Suddenly the answers didn't matter.

Sage turned, wrapped Deanne in her arms and pressed

her lips into her hair. "I'm sorry," she whispered, "I'm sorry."

Deanne nodded gently, snugged her arms around Sage's back and held her tightly. "I wanted to tell you I was sorry," she said softly, "the minute you walked out the door."

"It's okay."

"I was so sure you'd left me. You haven't, have you?"

Sage relaxed her embrace, gently cupped Deanne's chin and turned her face upward. "No, baby," she said, and kissed her salty cheek. "No." She continued to kiss the wetness from Deanne's cheeks. "Please forgive me."

"It wasn't about having children. It was about shutting me out, about not trusting my judgment and my loyalty, about not being important enough. I'll help you raise as many babies as you want. I would have them for you if I could."

"I know you would, out of love for me. And you were right. I haven't been fair to you. I've never had to ask. I've always had to decide what was best for me in my life. And good or bad, I've been the only one who had to live with my decisions. I didn't realize that now I'm expecting you to live with them without having any say in them. I'll try not to do that anymore."

"Just put your arms around me. Then I know everything is going be all right." She leaned into Sage's embrace and felt the reassurance of her arms around her. "I realized something else, too. I can't measure your intimacy by my measuring stick. That's not fair either."

"Then we're okay?"

"Yes," Deanne whispered. "Oh yes."

Sage kissed Deanne's forehead and then the side of her face. "It's good to be home."

Deanne tightened her arms around Sage's waist. "I want to be here more than anywhere else, and not because it's beautiful. I would be with you in a trailer park or a one-room apartment. Anywhere, as long as we're together."

"You're never going to get less than my best," Sage said into Deanne's uplifted face. "I promise you that."

"All I've ever needed is the best of your heart."

She lifted her lips to Sage's, and welcomed the warmth and tenderness of them. Under their lids, her eyes watered into tears. She was weak. How could she be so happy and so weak at the same time? The stronger the love, the weaker the resistance against it? If only she could believe Sage was this weak for her.

Sage's lips widened into a grin. Deanne opened her eyes just as a purring ball of fur pushed a wet nose against her cheek. The kitten had deftly made her way from the deck to the table to the railing and onto Sage's right shoulder, no doubt thinking *how could they have forgotten to greet the most important member of the household? Who did they think kept everything in order while they were busy falling apart? Pillows needed hollows pressed into their centers. Toilet paper needed to be unrolled. Unread magazines needed to be cleared from the coffee table. It had been a tough week. A little appreciation was in order.*

Sage blew gently into the oversize ear tickling her nose and received a head butt on the chin. "Have you behaved yourself?" she asked as the kitten kneaded a nest between their chests.

"How could you doubt such cherublike innocence?" Deanne kissed the furry face rubbing white whiskers across her chin. "She's been trying to train me all week. I'm a slow learner."

"That's hard to believe."

"Ask her," she said, smiling though the last of the tears still rolling from the corners of her eyes.

Sage cleared the remaining wetness from Deanne's face with her thumbs.

"I forgot to put the toilet paper on the roller backward. So she reminded me by showing me how far someone with a little patience could unroll it. Go ahead, tell her," Deanne directed to the innocently blinking aqua eyes. "Out of the bathroom, down the hallway, one continuous white trail, unbroken, down the stairs, and across the kitchen." She was laughing now with Sage. "She's sure I won't forget again."

"Such a tough job," Sage said with a playful frown, "training your humans."

"And I kept forgetting her treats. So she figured out how to get to the top of the refrigerator and open the cupboard and help herself."

"That's my girl," she said with a wide smile.

"And she'll still be your girl when she's throwing a hissy fit on the other side of the bedroom door tonight."

"No threesomes, huh? Even if she promises to keep her licking to herself?"

Deanne placed the still purring ball of fluff on the floor

and returned her arms to Sage's waist. "No boys, no toys." She added coyly, "no kittens."

"I see," she winked. "Just me."

"Just you." Deanne brought her hand around to place the palm over the front of Sage's jeans. "That is until there's a baby we can't leave on the other side of the bedroom door."

"I've decided to hold my last trump card."

Deanne's eyes widened with surprise. "Is Cimmie pregnant?"

Sage shook her head. "But there's more to Jeff than either of us realized. He's not afraid to make a family that society has no parameters for. Cimmie's going to try *in vitro*."

Deanne felt as if she'd suddenly been filled with helium, and she expressed her relief with a tight hug. "Sometimes when you loosen the tension, things fall right into place." She looked into Sage's eyes. "We both need to get better at that."

Sage nodded. As a child, she could ride a bike no handed down the steepest hills, through the heaviest traffic. As an adult she would have to learn to ride as fearlessly on the back of someone else's bike.

"Preparing for the *in vitro* procedure is going to be a long process. A week of gonadotropin injections to stimulate my ovaries. Another week of monitoring and tests and maybe more injections before they harvest the eggs." Sage knew the answer before she asked, "Will you come to New York and be with me?"

"I'd be there even if you didn't ask."

Chapter 19

"Did you read all the information the nurse gave you?" The question was asked methodically. Only the nest of red-brown curls covering Doctor Kamden's head was visible as she dutifully covered the questions on her checklist.

"Yes, I read it all carefully," replied Sage.

"And you realize that there is no guarantee that this procedure will ultimately result in pregnancy."

"A fifty-percent chance for the first attempt. But at thirty-five, my eggs are borderline."

The doctor looked up from her paperwork. "I'm used to people saying they read it but believing only what they want to believe."

Suddenly worthy of the doctor's serious eye contact, Sage waited for her to continue.

"This has been a physical and emotional roller coaster for Cimmie, and this may not smooth it out. There could be more failures, and you may just be hopping on that roller coaster with her."

Sage offered no expression and no indication that that would deter her.

The doctor continued. "Although egg retrieval by using ultrasonography is much less invasive that laparoscopy, it is still uncomfortable at best. At its worst it's quite painful."

"I'm sure I've felt worse."

"Hmm," Dr Kamden contemplated. "Nevertheless we hope to extract enough eggs so that we don't have to do this again. We need enough eggs so that after fertilization we'll end up with eight or nine healthy embryos. Four of those will be transferred on the first attempt. The others will be frozen for another attempt."

"And if the second one doesn't take, we'll have to do this again."

"Yes. Now, before fertilization of the eggs, we'll do a micro-sort of fresh sperm, as I explained to you before. By separating the female-producing sperm and introducing only those sperm to the eggs we have a ninety-three percent chance of the embryos being female."

All the angles had been covered. Everything that was humanly and scientifically possible to assure that Cimmie would bear a female child was being done. Sage sighed an unconscious sigh of relief.

The doctor continued. "Although I'm confident that Nurse Nelson is very thorough in preparing our patients, I always like to explain in more detail what I'll be doing before we get started. That way I can answer any last questions you may have."

"I am awake during this whole thing, aren't I?"

"I always recommend a light anesthesia along with the paracervical block, but you said you didn't want it."

"No, I want to be completely alert."

The doctor nodded. "I'll explain the procedure, and if you still want to go that route, we'll use only the paracervical block." She shuffled her papers together and closed the folder, then moved a stainless steel tray holding a series of needles into view on the counter.

"Like dental work, much of the pain involved is in the anesthetizing. In order to numb the nerves around the cervix and uterus, we have to inject a local anesthetic on each side of the cervix and into the upper part of the vagina that surrounds the cervix."

She picked up a long narrow probe and showed it to Sage. "That allows us to insert an ultrasound probe, like this one, into the vagina. This is the projector that will transmit the images of the ovarian follicles, which house the eggs, to the viewing monitor. Then I'll pass a needle through this sleeve alongside the probe, through the top of the vagina and into the follicles to remove the eggs. The whole process takes about thirty minutes."

"You'll let me know if you got enough eggs?"

"Have you changed your mind about being sedated?"

"No."

Dr. Kamden assured her, "Then you'll know as we go along."

"One last question," Sage added. "What would *my* chances be?"

"Pregnancy?" She watched Sage nod. "About the same as Cimmie's. They're your eggs. The chance for success depends on their health more than anything else. Besides, you aren't exactly built for childbirth. Your hips are too narrow. To avoid problems you would probably be facing a Cesarean delivery." The doctor offered a quick upward twitch of her lips, which would almost pass for a smile. "Unless you have no other option, Cimmie is the better candidate for a normal childbirth."

Sage nodded again. "Then let's get this over with."

"Do you want Deanne or Cimmie in the room?"

"No," Sage smiled. "You have your hands full dealing with one patient."

Chapter 20

The night was perfect. A hard, chilling rain kept late-night walkers off the streets, chased them into taxis, and sent them home early. The hooded figure, bent against the rain as it streaked through elongated cones of streetlight, was unnoticed ducking into the brick front doorway.

No alarm sounded as the intruder entered the building and continued across the dimly lit waiting room, stumbled over the corner of a low table, and mumbled a curse into the silent room. The hallway, better lit with its low security lights, was more easily navigated. A series of doors, some solid and some with small glass windows, lined the hall, their doors closing their contents in darkness.

Office. Room A. B. Cold Storage. Laboratory. A gloved hand tried the knob to the laboratory. Locked. Fifteen seconds later it was open, and within minutes every petri dish and test tube—and anything else that looked like it may contain matter pertinent to the science of making babies—was smashed to the floor.

"And the science gods topple from their thrones"—the intruder's arm swept the last counter clear—"like the false prophets that they are."

The door to the adjoining cold storage room was unlocked. Swiftly latch after latch was jerked open, and the hopes and dreams of uncounted infertile couples were thrown to the floor and destroyed in a matter of seconds. The names—Gerard, Lancome, Thompson, Bristo—didn't matter now. The futures of hopeful parents were crunched into the fragments of glass underfoot.

The intruder took a wide black marker from a jacket pocket and wrote his message on the wall. *Leave to God that which is God's.*

The office was the last stop, and the scene of the final act of destruction. With a large magnet he placed his evil curse on the clinic computer system and dumped file boxes full of disks and paper files into a large basket. *We will stop you. Only God decides who will have children. You will not make babies for gays to raise, or clone homosexuals so that they can populate the earth.* He struck a match and held it to a paper's edge. The intruder waited, motionless, until flames filled the basket, then he slipped through the door and vanished in the rain.

Chapter 21

The tone of her voice was pitched high, out of control; the words strained through the top range of Cimmie's cries. "Our babies are dead," were the first words out of her mouth. The rest were undecipherable.

Sage spoke deliberately into the phone as she moved slowly across the kitchen toward Deanne. "Cim, take a deep breath. Come on, Cim, take a breath with me . . . I know you're trying. A deeper breath. Let it out slowly . . . Okay, I'm right here. Where's Jeff? . . . Okay, okay, I won't hang up until he gets home."

The look of concern in Sage's eyes drew Deanne to her side. She slipped her arm around her waist and looked intently into her eyes as Sage listened.

"They're all gone, Sage," Cimmie finally managed. "The babies are all dead."

"Take another breath, Cim, and tell me what happened, slowly."

There was an audible, shaky attempt on the other end to do what was asked. Then, "It was on the news today when I got home. Someone broke into the clinic."

Sage closed her eyes and clenched her jaw tight. She had wanted so badly for the awful feeling that had haunted her day and night for the past week to be nothing but the uneasiness of not having total control of things. It was clear now that ignoring it hadn't changed why it had been there.

Cimmie continued, her voice soft and weepy. "There's nothing left."

"You're sure? Did you talk to someone from the clinic?" Her thoughts reluctantly went to hormone injections and probes and embryos and doing it all over again.

"Who would do something like that?"

"A crazy. A fanatic. It only takes one."

"But why? We're not aborting babies." She sniffed and there was silence for a moment while she apparently wiped her nose. "We're trying to *have* babies."

"Who knows what goes on in the head of a crazy, Cim." She acknowledged the question in Deanne's eyes.

Deanne whispered, "Were the embryos destroyed?"

Sage nodded and continued into the phone. "All I know is that they're afraid, and that means you don't know what they're going to do."

Deanne squeezed her arms around Sage's waist. "I'm sorry," she whispered. Then she tucked her head under Sage's arm and rested it on her shoulder close to the phone where she could hear the other end of the conversation.

Cimmie's voice was still somewhat shaky. "Afraid of what? I don't understand."

"Afraid of science. We're not making babies according to Hoyle. Science isn't answering their moral standards. Or maybe they thought the clinic was experimenting with cloning."

Cimmie released a defeated breath that ended with the whine of an exhausted cry. "But they killed our baby."

"We'll start over, Cim. I'll call the doctor in the morning and find out when I can start the injections again."

Deanne closed her eyes and squeezed Sage tightly. What she and Cimmie were about to face again would stop many infertile couples right now, either emotionally or financially. The extent to which Sage was willing to go was apparent. But Deanne could hear the voice on the other end faintly sounding the white flag.

"I can't, Sage. I can't take any more. I think this is the last sign that it isn't meant to be."

Deanne took the phone. "Cimmie? We'll be there as soon as Sage gets a new schedule from the doctor. I'm going to stay with you while Sage goes through the injections. We'll get through this, I promise. We'll do it together. Okay?"

"Oh, Dee. You don't know what this is doing to me." She sounded weak, her voice fading. "I'm not me anymore."

It was true. It had happened so gradually that no one else had noticed. "Okay." Deanne relented. "But I want to come and be with you anyway. It's not any easier to accept defeat. That's something I have firsthand experience in. I'll see you soon. I love you. Here's Sage."

She covered the phone with her hand and spoke to the frown on Sage's face. "It's time you let me be a part of this family. And it's time that you loosened the tension." Her tone softened. "Don't embrace her so tightly. Just let her know that you love her."

Sage took the phone. The fold between her brows relaxed slightly. She nodded with a little smile and kissed Deanne's cheek. She'd be riding the back of that bike again, and it hadn't gotten any more comfortable.

Chapter 22

Once again in New York, Deanne indeed became an intrinsic part of the situation. During the three mental health days that Cimmie took from work, Deanne was her constant companion. While Sage reluctantly remained in Michigan and Jeff continued teaching, she went about coaxing back the Cimmie she'd first met almost five years ago.

They cooked strange recipes like Romanian Chicken Pancakes and Tigeroni and Hamburger Corn-Pone Pie, and tried them out on Jeff. They rented John Candy movies and ate popcorn and licorice sticks. Today they went junkin', spending hours scouring the second hand stores for fifties' memorabilia. And they never once discussed children.

"Don't tell Sage that I didn't make you wear latex gloves while we pawed through all this stuff," Cimmie said with a smile. "She thinks these places are disgusting."

"That's why I brought this." Deanne produced a trial-size bottle of waterless hand cleaner from her pocket.

"Oh, and you have to scrub your nails when we get home. That *is* going to be the first question she asks you."

Deanne looked at the ends of her fingers, now nearly black with yester-year's dirt. Cimmie continued rummaging through an unsorted box of miscellaneous items on the floor. She couldn't remember her mother's hands ever looking dirty like this. It wasn't until she was in high school that she knew where the clothes and other household items came from. Home, sick from school, she watched her mother match buttons, replace zippers, and wash and iron and fold like new the clothes she pulled from an unmarked garbage bag.

"I don't believe it. Look!" she exclaimed, holding up her treasure for Deanne to examine.

It was a clear juice-size glass, with no cracks or chips or noticeable scratches.

"What is it?" Deanne asked.

"Here, look," she directed, tipping the glass so that Deanne could see words and a girl's face embossed on the bottom.

"Princess Summerfall Winterspring. It's a *Howdy Doody* jelly glass. We used to have these when we were kids. How do you even know what this is? The TV show was off the air before you were even born."

"There was a collector who Grandma knew, and she would take us there sometimes on the weekends. He would play the old black-and-white TV shows for us, and

I fell in love with Howdy. He was so cute in his little jeans and boots. And I loved Clarabell and Mr. Bluster, and how Buffalo Bob treated them all like regular people. Sage liked the princess because she was an Indian. She had a beautiful singing voice. Judy Tyler, who played her, was killed in a car accident when she was only twenty-three."

"You're amazing," Deanne smiled. "You know more about my era than I do."

"Did you know that three days before she died, Tyler finished shooting *Jailhouse Rock* with Elvis Presley? It was the best film he ever made, and he wouldn't even go see it after she was killed."

"And now you have her glass."

"I sure do. And I'm going to get it for a quarter."

"How much is it worth?"

"You'd be shocked. How many of these do you think your mother threw out when you were kids?"

"You mean how many did we kids break. They were our juice glasses."

"This is worth some bucks. But I won't sell it. It was the only one of the set I didn't have."

"God, my mother would pee her pants."

"Say, kids! What time is it?" Cimmie giggled, working her way happily around used bikes and racks of clothes toward the counter.

Outside the store, Deanne made them both use the waterless cleaner before they started home.

"I would want my kids to see shows like *Howdy Doody*

and *Captain Kangaroo*. Oh, did you know that Robert Keeshan, the Captain, was the original Clarabell?"

Deanne just shook her head and chuckled.

"They should see clean, nonviolent humor, shows that teach respect and tolerance. I guess *Barney* is okay, but there is so much junk. I would be the pickiest mother on earth." She stopped walking and took Deanne's arm. "I do want kids."

Deanne looked into eyes as large and dark as Sage's and waited.

"Do you think I should try again?"

"Yes," Deanne said with a nod.

"I wish you didn't have to go back tomorrow. Why don't you call Sage and tell her you're going to stay Saturday and get a flight back Sunday?"

"I was hoping you'd ask me. There was another recipe I saw in that book that I think we ought to try. I don't think we've tortured Jeff nearly enough yet."

Chapter 23

Nothing was left to chance. Arrangements were made for the doctor to work out of another clinic, and Sage hired a private security company for around-the-clock security.

It took another week of injections, another painful extraction, and two more sperm sorts and *in vitro* attempts. But at last Cimmie was pregnant—gloriously and wonderfully pregnant.

No special glow to speak of, Deanne thought, watching Cimmie amid the bustle of activity in Sharon's basement. She smiled and opened presents, but she looked tired. Even the usual glow that surrounded the wide, bright eyes and Shirley Temple smile had faded. The umber of her skin tone had paled. Retained fluid puffed her face and sagged the skin under her eyes. The roller-coaster ride had taken its toll. However relieved she was emotionally, physically Cimmie was tired.

Sage, however, sparkled like newly poured spumante. She smiled often, and with a natural ease. Deanne watched her introducing her family, interacting with friends, and she saw a happiness in her face that she hadn't seen before. And the longer she watched her, the happier she felt herself.

"Okay, so I never imagined myself hosting a baby shower, either. It's kinda like visualizing me having sex with a man," Sharon announced with a sardonic grin. "But here I am, bigger than shit, toasting breeders."

Deanne leaned toward Jeff and Cimmie as they raised their glasses. "You were prewarned."

"Yes," Cimmie said and smiled. "By you *and* Sage."

"To a healthy baby girl"—Sharon looked over her glass at Cimmie—"there's no alcohol in that glass, is there?"

Cimmie shook her head. "No, Mother Superior."

Sharon cocked her head and continued. "And to her parents." She swung her glass to include Sage and Deanne. "All of them."

With smiles and agreement, the women joined in drinking their toast. Then Sage stood, turned to face Cimmie and Jeff, and raised her glass again. "To the continuation of the *Hodinon'deoga'*, a very old family, and the beginning of a new one."

Once again they sipped from their glasses. But before anyone else could add to the toast, Sharon downed her drink and announced loudly, "Okay, let's party."

Deanne raised her eyebrows at Jeff and Cimmie. "I told you this would not be your traditional baby shower."

"And I, for one, am glad it won't be," Jeff replied.

"You might want to reserve judgment until later in the evening," Sage remarked. "You're celebrating with a roomful of dykes, remember."

While music wove its way around conversations and all manner of sweets and treats were being consumed, the basement was being transformed into what looked suspiciously like an obstacle course.

Laura struggled to squeeze both herself and a tub of water through the kitchenette doorway. Jeff relieved her of her burden and was directed to place it at one end of a six-foot table. Sharon had already placed another tub at the other end.

"What's all this?" he asked.

"Something Sharon lay awake nights giggling over," Laura returned. "An event, she is sure, that is destined to go down in Dyke Olympic history. I love her, but sometimes she worries me," she added with a chuckle.

"All right," Sharon announced in her no-need-for-a-microphone voice, "enough sweet talk and junk food. It's time to show your true grit." She directed her attention to Jeff. "I guarantee you, mister, you are not the underdog here."

A quick look around them and it became apparent to everyone that traditional shower games had succumbed to Sharon's somewhat twisted idea of fun. There were props placed strategically down one side of the room and duplicated on the other. Baby dolls, diapers, car seats, and a smirk on Sharon's face promised nobody was going to get out of this one unscathed.

"Aw, Sharon," groaned Kasey.

"Laura, I thought you had better control than this," Sage added.

"I've learned to pick my battles. This one lost out to moving her beer can collection out of the bedroom."

"Oh, quit your grumbling. Everyone off your tushes, except for Mama Bear."

"I don't get to play?" Cimmie asked with an impish frown.

"Nope. Even when we even out the handicap," Sharon exaggerated the size of her own belly and gave it a pat, "you'll beat this bunch hands down. Actually you could probably beat them with no hands." She pulled a black-and-white striped pullover from a bag and a stopwatch from her pocket, and handed them to Cimmie. "You, my dear, along with myself, will officiate this fiasco."

"What do you mean by 'even out the handicap'?" Wendy asked suspiciously.

"Oh, so glad you asked. Laura was just about to demonstrate that very thing. Weren't you, dear?"

Laura's grin, overstated and unseen by Sharon, brought the laughter that was intended. Sharon turned to find Laura innocently grappling with the straps to a strange-looking piece of apparel with breasts and a pronounced belly. Sharon circled behind her and pulled the Velcro straps in place.

"You've got to be kidding." Kasey looked over at Sage.

"Looks like you are gonna get a hint of what it would've felt like."

"We," Sage returned. "*We* are going to get a hint."

"Okay, pay attention," Sharon ordered. "I'm only going through this once, then you're on your own." She stood in the middle of the room like a coach in the locker room at halftime. "You'll go two at a time. Laura's gonna strap you into this thing—which I guarantee will give you a whole new respect for Cimmie—then we have a few tasks for you to perform while we time how quickly you can complete them."

"Pregnant relays," Connie offered with a smile. "I hope someone's going to get pictures of this."

"Not to worry," Laura said. "You'll find disposable cameras under your chairs."

"Also under your chair is a number," Sharon added. "One and two, get your tushes up here."

Number one, who was at this very moment probably cursing her Murphy's Law luck, was Wendy Carnes. "Ms. Efficiency" on or off the job, she immediately picked up the instruction card next to the child safety seat and began reading it.

Sharon immediately snatched the card away and slapped her hand.

Number two was a still-grumbling Kasey. "Have I missed something," she said, "or have you not given us any reason to totally embarrass ourselves?"

"Yeah, yeah," Sharon rummaged in her shopping bag and produced two envelopes. "The laughs I'm gonna get outta this are worth dangling a couple of big juicy carrots."

She held up one envelope. "Runner-up wins an Eddie Bauer gift certificate." Then the second one. "The winner gets two floor tickets to the Detroit Shock's home opener."

"Oh yeah." Kasey burst forward to stand next to Sharon. "I can be real embarrassed for those."

"If you're through whining, I'll explain this." Sharon bent over, emptied the two laundry baskets and scattered the clothes on the floor. "This one's self-explanatory."

Then she moved to the table that held the two tubs of water and two lifelike baby dolls. "Wash your baby from head to toe, dry her, powder her . . ." With a grin she held up a little outfit with hands and feet and a hundred snaps. "And dress her."

She moved on, baby doll in hand, to a rocking chair. "Now, since it's not possible to actually feed this baby . . ." Sharon sat in the chair and cradled the doll with one arm. Laura handed her a baby bottle of milk. "You're going to have to rock the baby until you finish off this sucker yourself."

Amidst the rumblings, Laura held up a bottle filled with water. "This one's for Deanne, so don't anyone else take it."

"Okay," Sharon tossed the baby doll to Laura. "The last thing you have to do is figure out how to strap the little bugger into the safety seat. May the best," she made a dismissive gesture with her hand, "whatever, win."

Laura strapped up her first two contestants, who were immediately met with a barrage of camera flashes. Then, as the contestants fumbled their way through improbable motherhood, the cameras continued clicking to an accompaniment of laughter.

And there was plenty to laugh at. While Kasey worked her way through her tasks like a classic Saunders-run through a tight defense, Wendy encountered problem after problem. Slippery when wet, her baby doll slipped from her grip and bounced under the table, where in her haste to stand up Wendy drove the top of her head painfully up into its edge. Her poor finish time became irrelevant when, out of frustration, she took the nipple off the bottle to gulp its contents and disqualify herself.

The laughter reached near hysterics when Ali, not wanting to put her acrylic nails in water, held the wash cloth between thumb and forefinger and passed it over the doll that she held dangling by one arm over the tub.

"Oh, shut up," Ali snipped with a look of disgust. "Like I'd really baby-sit the little ankle-bite anyway."

Her time was running so long that she was still trying to force dry clothing over a wet baby when Deanne finished her bottle of water through fits of laughter and easily snapped her baby into the car seat. At that point Ali picked her doll up by one arm, its clothes hanging from one leg, dropped it carelessly into the car seat and continued to her chair. She ripped loose the Velcro straps herself, and dropped the pregnancy contraption onto Sage's lap.

"*This*," she said with a sultry smile, "is what *I've* been waiting for."

As were the others. The only two still to make fools of

themselves were Jeff and Sage. They rose to cheers and moved to the other side of the room, where Sage leaned over and whispered something in Jeff's ear.

Neither of them turned around to face the awaiting laughter until both were strapped into temporary pregnancy. Then, together, they turned to strike twin Demi-style poses, and endure the expected barrage of snapshots. A picture no child under the age of thirty would claim as her parents.

Sharon was doubled in laughter. "Oh my god," she exclaimed. "I've outdone myself. It was all worth it for this one moment."

But the two were undaunted. "What's the time to beat?" Jeff asked.

"Kasey's," answered a more-in-control Laura. "Three-eighteen."

The stopwatch started, and Jeff bent to pick up the clothes. He groaned loudly as the strategically placed weighted balls sewn into the belly pressed painfully against his bladder.

Sage tipped the basket on end and without bending pushed the clothes into it with her foot. Then she moved swiftly to the bathing table.

"She has a whole new approach to housework," Connie said with a chuckle.

"You should see her dry dishes," Deanne added. "Of course, there is no logical reason to actually *dry* dishes you understand, but when I insist, she waits until all the plates are washed, takes the whole stack at once and dries them like they're a stack of cards—the top of the one on top, the bottom of the one on the bottom, then shuffles the top plate to the bottom of the stack, and so on until they're all dry."

Connie shook her head and smiled, then leaned over Deanne and spoke so that Cimmie could hear her. "How did those two get paired up?"

Baby powder was everywhere, the table, the floor, Jeff, Sage—and water as well, but not as easily seen. Sage had dried her baby doll and was applying powder when it started. A second after Jeff realized she was halfway around the table and leading, his washcloth loaded with water splatted on top of Sage's doll.

"I see you need help," she said, sending powder flying over his doll and everything else in its path.

"Thanks so much," he returned, grabbing her baby's outfit and flinging it across the room.

Cimmie froze the comedy for prosperity with a click of the camera. "Without proof," she said, "no one is going to believe Jeff did this. I don't think he would have if Sage hadn't."

"They are a pair. And not one I ever would have guessed," added Deanne. She grabbed the stitch in her side, but continued to laugh as Sage, who had been squeezing the bottle and squirting the milk into her mouth, sent a long squirt to her left and hit Jeff right in the face.

"Is that any way to treat a pregnant man?" He frowned and returned a shot of milk that continued the battle that should have disqualified them both.

But Sharon wasn't about to end the fun prematurely. She

let them duck and squirt and drench each other until the bottles were empty and everyone had gotten the pictures that no doubt would reach the outmost boundaries of the lesbian community.

It was no surprise when the two of them plunked their babies into the car seats, snapped the buckles in place and ended the relay in a dead heat.

"Please tell me," Sage said, milk dripping from her hair and baby powder freckling her face, "that this doesn't mean we have to go shopping together."

"No. You can do a tiebreaker," Sharon returned. "Watching this fiasco gave me some great ideas. They're disturbing enough to make me worry about *myself*."

"If you think there's any chance of *that*," Jeff replied, motioning for Laura to unstrap him, "I obviously look as stupid as I feel."

"Oh no. Not at all." Sage palmed the belly of her contraption as Deanne unfastened it. "How about a game of one-on-one?"

Chapter 24

"Lena, come here. You should see this."

Reluctantly, Lena laid the bookmark in place, right before the page that surely was about to disclose the most important clue to the mystery disappearance of the chocolate heiress, and left her book on the chair.

"Are you coming? I don't want you to miss this."

"Yes, John," she replied, without much hope that what he wanted her to see would lift her spirits or make her smile. It had been a long time since he'd offered anything that did that. "What is it?" she asked as she entered the inner sanctuary of their home.

As expected, John was stationed in his leather wingback chair, a cigarette burning in the ashtray next to him. Sometimes when she looked at him, she could still see the man with the courtship eyes. The one who had shown her the world of Rome and Venice and Paris. It wasn't often, but every now and then, something he would say, or maybe the way he said it, would lift the years from his face and she could see the pleasure her love once gave him. The boyish excitement at showing her things she'd never seen, the pride he felt at her being by his side. It was enough that she knew they were there.

With the remote he motioned toward the television.

Lena settled onto the end of the couch just as the newsmagazine reporter began the substance of her report.

"Recently, there has been a lot of media attention being paid to the discovery of a gay gene. Tonight we will be speaking with a professional in the field of genetic research to sort out fact from fiction concerning this controversial subject."

The chocolate heiress would have to wait. Lena tucked her legs up under her and resolved to listen to the whole program. She would rather hear it firsthand than endure John's rendition later. It was easy for the facts to take on a certain slant in his head, and difficult for her to determine later what was fact and what was his interpretation.

"They're talking about some of the findings of Dean Hamer," John explained over the reporter's voice. "That was the book Jeremy sent me that I wanted you to read."

Which she had attempted to do, but had tired too quickly of the scientific rhetoric. It was easy to see how the findings could be controversial. They were confusing, and she found it hard to know what to make of them. She sighed and rested her head against the back of the couch, and wished she could be in the other room finishing her mystery.

"The CBS-*New York Times* poll showed that the majority of Americans," the reporter was saying, "would be more inclined to accept homosexuality if they were convinced it was an inborn trait, rather than a choice. Do you think recent findings in genetic research are that convincing?"

The doctor being interviewed, whose name Lena hadn't heard, looked genuinely hopeful. "I think they will go a long way in that direction. But first, I must clarify that there is no evidence that points to a singular gay gene being responsible for sexual orientation. And second, it's important to keep in mind that Hamer himself is quoted as saying that it is 'very dangerous to mix biology and genetics with legal, social, and ethical concerns.' We need to withhold judgment until more results are available from studies of larger samples. To this point, the studies have been limited to a very narrow group of people."

"And don't some of the results conflict one another, especially regarding lesbians?"

"Again I caution you against giving too much weight to these conclusions until more research is available, but yes, there do seem to be some contradictory findings."

The reporter, anxious to show that she had done her homework, continued. "The research from the University of Texas on lesbian hearing seemingly contradicts the work of Michael Bailey and Nicholas Martin which contends that sexual orientation in women does not have a genetic component."

"Yes. The study in Texas found that lesbian hearing is more like a man's hearing, in that it is less sensitive to slight sounds than that of heterosexual women. They suggested that this could be due to exposure to male hormones before birth. And, if we accept their conclusion that the auditory center of a lesbian has been masculinized, and therefore so have the brain sites that direct sexual preference, then it makes it hard to accept a study that finds lesbian sexuality to be based more on environment than genetics."

John drew on his cigarette and turned his head to exhale away from Lena. He seemed unaffected by the apparent conflict of information, and continued to listen.

Exactly how he expected *her* to relate this information, Lena wasn't sure. She was sure, of course, that it had everything to do with Sage, and somehow, that it must support her husband's view that her daughter was a menace to society. Otherwise, there would be no need to share it with her. It wasn't like John to point out something that would undermine his stand.

"Professionally, with everything that you know about both areas of research, what do you think we're going to find, let's say, in the next ten years?"

The doctor hesitated thoughtfully. "With the tremendous slowdown in research lately, it is unfortunately more realistic to think about things in terms of more than ten years down the road. Eventually, though, I'm sure we're going to find that the two areas work in concordance with each other."

"In other words," the reporter concluded, "both findings have validity."

"Yes, I believe that. There are unmistakable genetic components, or markers, that work in a complex conspiracy to shape sexual tendencies. And the effects of socialization on human behavior have been well documented for years. The hard part is understanding how they interact with one another. Then maybe we'll be able to accept that a boy from rural Kansas, where he has experienced virtually no gay influence, can end up gay, and that a lesbian can be married to a man for years before realizing her true sexual orientation."

Then, just as Lena's mind was beginning to sort through the clues to the missing heiress, the reporter made the connection that John wanted her to hear. "I don't mean to sound contrary, but don't you think it is going to be more difficult to accept the idea of homosexuals having children when that means they will be passing on their homosexual genes to their children?"

"That is one of the conclusions that Dr. Hamer warned against linking to ethical or moral concerns."

"But a lot of people will probably make that link."

"Probably."

John Capra, of course, was one of those people. Lena understood now why he had been so interested in the fertility drugs. It wasn't *if* but *how* Cimmie became pregnant that he was concerned with.

The program had moved on to the next segment, and John clicked off the set. "Do you see what I've been saying?" he asked. "They will pass their sickness on, one way or another."

"But the scientists are still speculating, they—"

He stood and snuffed out his cigarette. "How can you be so naïve?"

Chapter 25

"We don't need anything, Mom." Cimmie eased herself down onto the couch with an audible groan into the phone. "No, I'm fine. I'm beginning to think our species shouldn't have evolved this far. Walking on all fours has got to feel better than anything I've tried so far."

She looked longingly at the glass of ice water on the coffee table but decided against disturbing her semi-satisfactory lean into the couch pillows. "No, we have so many clothes that I'll be able to change her five times a day and still not run out . . . We don't need to go shopping, Mom . . . Okay, why don't I meet you for lunch."

Cimmie made herself as comfortable as she could, turning her chair slightly to the side in order to sit closer to the table. She looked across at her mother, with her eyeglasses low on the bridge of her nose, glancing over a menu she knew by heart. It wasn't surprising that

Lena would pick Raos's for their lunch. Italian, family-owned for a century, with a bartender named the Vest who knew her by her first name. Of course they would come here.

And why not? Cimmie thought. *We must keep Mom in her comfort zone.* Cimmie, the Peacemaker, would have it no other way—especially now, with hormone levels running the gamut and emotions ricocheting like a super ball in a handball court. Today, it might be the best she could offer. This first conversation in months was destined to go beyond chitchat, and her promise to Sage was all but broken already.

Cimmie took a deep breath as the waiter disappeared with their orders.

"Are you all right?" Lena asked.

"I'm fine," she said, taking a sip of water. *If I can ignore this horrible urge to bolt from this table, to get safely home and to close the door . . . It's going to be fine. I know how to get through this. Deep breaths . . . deeper breaths. My heart will slow down. Nothing bad is going to happen.* Cimmie looked hard at her mother, concentrated on the slightness of her stature, the soft roundness of her eyes. *Remember she has felt fear too. There is nothing to be afraid of.*

She took another sip of water and cleared her throat. "I've been asked that question more in the past eight months than I have in all my thirty-three years." A statement she was sure Lena would let lie and step lightly around as if it were never uttered.

"I found a beautiful set of furniture for the baby's room . . . "

Couldn't you prove me wrong, just once?

" . . . solid cherry. It has a changing table with lots of storage underneath. The dresser has six drawers, and the crib—"

"Mom, we can't afford it."

"Your dad and I want to get it for you. Our present for the baby."

"No, Mom. Jeff made a beautiful maple cradle that will be fine for the first few months, and his sister gave us a crib that's in great shape."

"What do you need?" Lena said, without a clue of what she had just asked.

Cimmie stabbed at the contents of her salad with no real intent to eat it. "I don't think you do want to know that. I've tried to tell you for years, but you only hear what you want to hear."

Lena's focus dropped abruptly to her plate. "Don't ruin our lunch, Cimmie," she said without looking up.

"You're never going to face it, are you?" Cimmie watched her mother pour another glass of water and continue to avoid her eyes. "Don't you see? It has to start with you."

"I don't know what you want from me." Lena's eyes met Cimmie's only briefly. "Your father worked hard. I made sure you had everything. You never appreciated that."

"You're right, I didn't." Cimmie reached absently for her glass. The heel of her hand caught the top of the glass and sent the water sloshing to the very edge of the rim. Suddenly

145

it was a glass of milk, and she was six or seven and it was spilling across the dinner table. She was crying as her mother grabbed napkins to stop the flow at the edge of the table and scurried off for a towel to clean up the mess. And her father's voice boomed its reprimand while Sage scrambled from her chair to wedge herself between Cimmie and the next stinging blow from her father's hand. She knew even then that the demands of an eight-year-old to "leave her alone" should have been coming from her mother. Instead, the demands tipped the edge for John Capra and sent a bruised and defiant Sage to her closet prison once again.

Cimmie stared at her water glass. It was upright, her hand securely around it. Lena was thanking the waiter for her plate of manicotti.

"Are you sure you're all right, Cimmie? You look a little pale."

Cimmie nodded almost unnoticeably. "I was remembering spilling milk on the dining room table. Do you remember that?"

"You kids were always spilling something," Lena offered between bites. "Here, taste this," she said, dropping a forkful of manicotti on the edge of Cimmie's plate.

"Sometimes I think therapy brings back more than it takes away."

"I don't know why you waste your money on that. You have a good life. Lots of friends, a good man. You put too much faith in psychologists. I think they do more harm than good."

"Well, that's one thing you and Sage think exactly alike on." She watched the expression in her mother's face dissolve, the corners of her eyelids and the lines that parenthesized her mouth droop vacuously. "Are you going to go to your grave without resolution, like you let NaNan?"

"There's nothing I can do about that."

"Yes there is, Mother. You could stand up for once and make a decision of your own. Look in the mirror and say it out loud. You could take responsibility for not doing it before. Start by telling Sage that you love her."

Lena dabbed at the corners of her mouth with her napkin, then smoothed it once again over her lap. She broke off another piece of the house-made bread without a reply.

"It's the only thing we really needed. You've never been able to tell us that."

The chunk of bread stalled in a pool of olive oil, and Lena's eyes flashed up to meet Cimmie's. "Yes, I have," she replied with a tone mixed with surprise and indignation.

Cimmie silently shook her head.

"Why do you say such things?" She added defensively, "I've always loved my children."

"Then how could you allow him to do that to us?"

"He's a nervous man. He needs peace and quiet. Having children was hard on him. I did the best I could to keep peace."

"So you walked on eggshells, and expected little children to as well?"

"I was the one who took care of you whenever you were sick." Tears formed in Lena's eyes. "I went to all your school functions. I saw to it that you had dance lessons, and music lessons"—she lowered her head and tried inconspicuously to blot the tears with her napkin—"and the latest clothes."

"You *don't* see, do you? It doesn't matter what I say, as long as it's covered so well with all the little niceties of my life. As long as I still talk to you and have lunch with you and accept your peace offerings, you can pretend everything's fine. But, what about Sage? How can you ignore what it did to her? She doesn't want me even talking to you. She doesn't trust you knowing that this baby is hers."

"She never listened to me. She always did things that infuriated him."

"She was just a little girl, Mother, and you know it's much more than that. Sage is hundreds of miles away, hasn't seen him or talked to him in years, and I'll bet just the sound of her name still infuriates him. Doesn't it?"

Lena slipped on her glasses. She concentrated on looking at the bill and extracting her billfold from her purse that was sitting on the floor.

Her ability to ride out a confrontation wasn't much greater than her husband's tolerance, but she had made it through longer than Cimmie had thought she would today. Cimmie had unloaded more this time than she'd been able to in previous years of trying. Her opportunity was about to end, but not before she got the last of it off her chest.

"She's a lesbian, Mother. Not a murderer. Not a thief. I doubt that she has broken any more of the Ten Commandments than you have. Haven't you ever lied? Or failed to honor your own mother? How about coveting something that belongs to another?"

"You shouldn't talk to me this way," Lena said softly as she laid thirty dollars on top of the bill.

"I'll stop when you can show me where in the Bible it says that God commands you to honor your husband's false judgment. You weren't given the right to judge her—only the right to love her."

Lena rose from the table, hints of her final line of defense obvious in the stiff hold of her head and the thin, straight line of her lips pressed tightly together. She was dousing herself in self-righteous pain.

"Now you're going to walk away because this makes you uncomfortable."

Lena hesitated at Cimmie's side and looked down at the lunch practically untouched in front of her.

"Go on, Mother. Go on back to your life. Cover all the ugly little edges with a nice plush carpet of denial. If you only knew how much Sage is like you. There's no hope for either of you."

Chapter 26

You wouldn't think that a woman who followed her day planner religiously would fly off to New York on merely a sudden feeling that she should be there.

Deanne relaxed her fingers momentarily, then tightened again and explosively pushed the grips to the chest press up and away from her body. Slowly she exhaled, counting to four as she lowered the weight for the eighth repetition of her third set. Her muscles burned. The last two reps would be nearly impossible. She inhaled deeply, tightened her grip again, and exploded upward as she exhaled. Three-quarters of the way up her arms shook with the tension. Aaaggghhh. The sound, wrenched up from her toes, forced the weight up the final few inches. She rested there a second, arms fully extended, before lowering it, then made shaky antagonist muscles suffer the four-count down again.

Deanne closed her eyes and immediately inhaled into the final explosion before her will gave in to the exhaustion of her muscles and convinced her that nine was enough today. Bright red and slick with perspiration, her quivering arms barely made the pinnacle of the final extension and started immediately down. She exhaled quickly—one, two, three, four. Her hands dropped to the floor like lead weights at the end of fishing line.

Impulsiveness is not a Bristo character trait, she thought, staring blankly at the ceiling of the basement workout room. *Sage has already been to the reservation this month, and Cimmie is fine; she said so just yesterday.*

The rain was falling steadily now, dripping through the deck boards above and making widening wet tracks on the bricks outside the patio doors. So much for her run today. She couldn't bring herself to spend even a half-hour on the treadmill. Michigan winters forced her to use it too many days as it was. *Maybe it will stop later.* And maybe with no interruptions today she could figure out some ingenious way to write around the obvious gap of information about Lena Capra. Not being able to finish the book clung like a stubborn tangle in the back of her mind.

She reached for the towel draped over the lat-pull bar just as a green blur flew from the stairs and bounced across the carpet. It was followed closely by a larger gray blur that grabbed up the toy in its mouth, raced across the room, leapt from the chair to the pool table, crossed the table with fur pantaloons flying, hit the back of the spectator bench with front paws then back paws, landed on the floor, and raced back up the stairs.

Still laughing, Deanne peeked around the corner of the

stairway. There on the landing the kitten lay, her green "baby," which no longer had eyes or whiskers or squeaker, clutched between her paws, and her pink-ribbon tongue hanging from her open mouth like a puppy's.

At the sight of Deanne, she snapped in her tongue, stood and slapped the toy again, sending it flying down the stairs and beginning the game all over. She was hilarious—ears back, running around her self-made racetrack, loose fur settling slowly in her wake on the green felt of the table.

Deanne peeked around the corner at her again. "Are you ever going to do this when Sage is home, or is this just for my entertainment?"

The toy flew past her again. "You have the energy of a two-year-old." Deanne chuckled to herself as she climbed the stairs.

"Okay. Check the e-mail," she muttered, entering the library. "Take a nice shower." She waited for the AOL screen. "And get to work."

"You have mail," the computer voice announced.

Deanne checked the messages. The daily hello from Mom. *"I'll never be able to remember how to use this thing."* But look at her now. A thank-you from Connie for the birthday gift. A reminder from Sharon that card night had been postponed until next week.

"Sequins and tails?" Wendy had forwarded the strange greeting from the office computer. The screen name was unfamiliar.

The message was simple and short and very disturbing. "May 20. Sequins and tails. I miss you."

Deanne sat for a moment staring at the screen. *Don't panic,* she cautioned herself. *This could be nothing.* But despite the caution and a deep breath, a poison burned its way toward the pit of her stomach.

She searched the AOL profiles for Tally2T and found nothing. *May 20.* She quickly checked the calendar. *Today. Who is this?*

She bolted from the library, ran to the master bedroom and flung open Sage's closet doors. Three walls of the huge walk-in were lined with neatly ironed shirts and pants and business suits. The black leather garment bag and overnighter were gone, but there, right where it always hung, was Sage's custom-tailored Armani tuxedo.

With a huge, audible sigh Deanne lifted the plastic bag and fingered the lines of the lapel. "You're here, you beautifully tailored thing. You're here."

Slowly she wandered back to the library, trying to reassure herself that this was only her own insecurity, based on things long ago and far removed from Sage, and wondering how far she should go to try to quell the remaining questions. So far her reactions had screamed mistrust so loudly that Sage could've felt their vibrations in New York.

One phone call. *Maybe it was an old friend of the family, an old business associate, maybe a political fundraiser. The message didn't say "love you." It said "miss you."*

She dialed the Longhouse office. "Wendy? Oh, fine, thanks. Hey, I just have a quick question. The e-mail you forwarded to Sage, did she get it before she left this morning?" *Stupid question,* she thought too late. *It wasn't marked as read. I'm grasping, and now Wendy knows it.*

"It wasn't marked as read?"

"Oh no. I'm sorry. How stupid."

"Not really," Wendy replied in her usual business tone. "That's one reason I forwarded it. It came in yesterday and wasn't marked yet this morning, so I sent it over. Sometimes Sage reads them, and if she doesn't have time to make a note, she keeps them as new mail as a reminder to herself later."

"I see. I was concerned that it may have been important, and she left with such short notice. Any idea who it's from?"

"Sorry, I don't. There's never any other name other than the screen name. That woman of yours needs a laptop."

"Yes," Deanne answered absently. *There've been other messages. But I can't ask how many. Enough.* "Thanks, Wendy. It's probably no big deal. I'll tell her when she calls tonight."

Chapter 27

"For you," Cimmie said, handing the phone to Sage. "It's Tia." She watched her sister rise from the couch and move discreetly toward the apartment's large sunlit window.

Sage continued speaking quietly, discreetly, until the door buzzer sounded. She motioned for Cimmie to stay seated, deposited the phone on the coffee table and answered the door.

"Are you sure you'll be okay alone tonight?" Sage made no eye contact as she untied the knotted bottom of the delivered garment bag. She lifted the plastic as Cimmie appeared beside her to hold the hanger, and removed the tuxedo.

"I'm pregnant, Sage, not terminal. And I'm going to be lugging this little tud-ball around for another three weeks. So why don't you tell me the real reason you're here?"

"Even you, Cim?" Eyes that since childhood had demanded her honesty bore into Cimmie's. "Why does it have to be more than a feeling that I should be here? You think it's about tonight, don't you? About Tia. Cimmie, it's a political fund-raiser, not a secret rendezvous." She wadded up the plastic and took the hanger from Cimmie. "It's not about Tia," she said curtly and left the room without waiting for an unnecessary reply.

All evening they moved through a sea of glitz and glitter, Tia on Sage's arm, working the ballroom like a runway. Hair pulled smoothly back from her face and turned neatly into a knot at the back of her neck showed off the bone structure that had caught many a photographer's eye. The short cocktail dress, with its open back and navel-length see-through V, turned even the heads of the men.

It was an evening of celebration for a year of steady political gains and of gratitude for contributions, big and small, toward another year of continued effort.

Sage showed her appreciation with a sizable contribution each year, but she hadn't attended a fund-raiser since she moved to Michigan. She couldn't explain why. In fact, she hadn't really thought about it. Building a business with the Longhouse, and their home, and tending to a relationship, had made her life drastically different than when she lived in New York. Being here tonight amid the movers and shakers, the motivators, and the politically influential brought back a feeling of inclusiveness. Here in New York she had been a part of all this. She had been aware, involved. Her opinions were sought after and respected, her organizational skills used and challenged.

It seems so long ago, Sage thought, looking into many familiar, and just as many unfamiliar, faces as they smiled their greetings and welcomed her back. *Has it really been only four years?* She'd meant to stay involved, but there had never seemed to be enough time.

"This is where you belong," Tia was saying, as they claimed a small round table near the edge of the dance floor. "Where your talents sparkle like white diamonds." She leaned close to Sage, her focus dropping to watch the long painted nail of her own index finger draw slowly down the pearl white studs of Sage's shirt. "And where you're appreciated for all you have to offer."

"Did I say I was offering?"

Long lashes lifted coyly. "You don't have to."

Sage cocked her head. "You're as presumptuous as ever."

"Presumptuous?" Tia said with a flippant smile. "You're here, aren't you?"

"Yes," Sage said as she stood. "To dance with an old friend"—she offered Tia her hand—"and because you needed an escort."

Tia welcomed the invitation, and the provocative sound of the jazz horns drawing her close into Sage's arms. "You're as light as down floating on a warm southern breeze," Tia said softly near Sage's ear. "Do you remember telling me that the first time we danced?"

"That was a long time ago."

"Is that what you tell your little author?"

"It's late," Tia said, approaching Sage's back as she stood before the counter of the large hotel-room bath. "You'll wake Cimmie if you leave now."

Sage finished drying her hands and straightened the towel still hanging on the bar. "How thoughtful you are."

Tia moved closer. "Look at us," she said, draping herself over the broad, straight shoulders like a toreador's cape. "We're beautiful together, tall and dark."

Sage glanced into the softly lit mirror only long enough to see what Tia wanted her to see—a pose for the ever-present camera, with her favorite dyke—then, turned her face nose-to-nose with Tia.

"Is it possible," Tia whispered, eyes half shielded with shimmering lids, "that you're the most handsome dyke I've ever had the pleasure of?"

"It is more likely," Sage whispered back, "that a night of wining, dining, and dancing is speaking louder than logic."

"Do you remember the night we first met?"

As clearly as this morning's trip. The memory, never actually far away, had been whispering to her throughout dinner and winking at her from across the dance floor. When she allowed it to dance freely across her conscious-ness, it curled the corners of her mouth and stirred an old familiar excitement. *How young we were then,* Sage thought, *but with masks to cover our naïveté already convincingly in place.*

A night like tonight. Full of glamour and excitement. A party that lured even the not-quite-out to celebrate a night with artists and designers and actors and musicians. It was a chance to meet the famous and the soon-to-be famous. And that night it included Tia, fresh off the runway and opening night of the new spring collection.

She was gorgeous. Sleek sophistication in a shimmering milk chocolate Versace. From the arm of her male model escort she toured the room as if it were a favorite country, sampling conversations here and tasting wine there. Gliding through the crowd with the poise of a princess, she appeared in small gatherings everywhere, until she had staked claim to the attention of practically everyone in attendance.

Sage was no exception. From the moment of Tia's arrival until the last turn of her head, Sage's gaze slipped past friends and wove around strangers to follow her movements. For her efforts she was rewarded with a smile and its promise of excitement and chestnut eyes that threatened to cast their spell.

The challenge seemed simple enough—look only long enough to be noticed, avoid long enough to entice. When it works she'll let you know—when it doesn't, *only* you know. Thus far, the successes had far outweighed the failures.

Sage watched for the signs that would invite an approach—a look that lingered too long, a smile aimed nowhere and responding to no one. Meanwhile, Sage sent signals of her own indicating that her date was that and no more. Her hand became no more familiar than the small of her date's back. She was attentive, but not exclusive. Her eyes never fell to the temptation to follow the curves of her date's body or to visit the glittered flesh filling the deep V of her dress. Self-discipline was imperative and until now had paid great dividends.

Tonight, however, her efforts had gone unnoticed. Others, men *and* women, were reaping the benefits of Tia's attention. They jockeyed for positions closest to her personal space and took impatient turns at impressing her.

There was no way of telling how impressed she really was. She engaged and dismissed one as graciously as another. None was shunned, none was favored. Then she left as she had arrived, on the arm of her escort.

And so did Sage. Home alone, she shed the confines of her tuxedo jacket and cummerbund and stripped to pants and loose-tailed shirt. Barefoot she padded across her apartment to the sounds of an early morning radio station to fix breakfast and ponder her failure.

A knock at the door at four AM was completely unexpected.

Visible in the circle of her door viewer was the profile that had graced the covers of *Glamour* and *Ebony* and *Vanity Fair*. Sage turned off the overhead light, suppressed a smile and opened the door.

"Good morning," Tia offered, entering the apartment without invitation.

Sage closed the door with a smile and a private acknowledgment at how wrong her assumption had been. When she turned, Tia's coat was laid across her arm, and Sage suddenly realized the aptness with which Tia had played the challenge. It stood now at a much higher level.

"You haven't asked if I'm alone," Sage remarked.

"*You* haven't asked why I'm here."

So began the power game between them, a game they soon both realized had no rules.

Sage deposited the coat on the arm of the sofa, motioned for Tia to sit down, and continued to a small bar in the corner of the living room. She mixed a martini, slightly on the dry side, proof of how observant she had been, and turned to hand it to Tia. To her surprise Tia was standing just behind her.

The dark center of Tia's eyes had widened in adjustment to the low lighting. They held the deeper dark of Sage's eyes in a captive gaze as two long fingers slid around the glass and removed it from Sage's hand.

"What is it you want, Sage Bristo?" Her lips touched the rim of the glass, but her eyes remained fixed on Sage's.

"To find what it is that pleases you."

"You'll get whatever you *really* want," she said, sipping from her drink, "if you can undress me without touching me."

The corners of Sage's mouth curled upward only slightly. She circled slowly to Tia's back before she allowed her eyes to travel the long sweeping curves still hugged elegantly in the sleek Versace. There were no visible hooks or clasps or zippers, only smooth uninterrupted material from her ankles to the narrow straps over her shoulders.

She continued circling, surveying, finding the slit that ran up the length of Tia's leg and stopped at the top of the shapely brown thigh.

Her eyes continued boldly as if searching out some flaw

161

that would make the challenge unworthy of the effort. They glanced over the narrow, protruding hips typical of a model, halted to study how perfectly arousing the shape of her breasts was—perfectly round, easily contained by an unstretched hand—pushing their button centers to definition beneath the soft material.

Over the rim of her glass, Tia watched the cool, dark eyes pass over her bare shoulders before finally returning to her own.

"What kind of music do you like, Tia?"

She tilted her head and stared for a second. "I doubt that I'll be here long enough to enjoy it."

Sage moved to the stereo with the nonchalance that she knew caused others a certain amount of anxiety. It made some, like her father, seethe with an anger in his gut that made her smile, and others, like the women in the clubs, squirm with a need they weren't comfortable with. Tonight she would find out how much anxiety it took to make a runway model squirm.

She selected two CDs. "Sade or Exposé?"

"Which has the shorter first selection?"

She chose Exposé. Her own preference, for her own reasons. And Sade would serve a different purpose.

"Why don't you refresh my drink? Waiting has a tendency to make me thirsty."

Sage did so, with the insouciance that had kept Tia at bay since her arrival, but making sure to touch her fingers under Tia's when she steadied the glass. All the while she denied Tia's eyes their demands, refused to meet them as if their magnificence had no effect whatsoever. Instead she tilted her head to the light so that Tia couldn't miss seeing the prominent line of her jaw, the deep set of her eyes, chiseled in shadow.

The sounds of Exposé danced around the room, surrounding Tia where she still stood, while Sage disappeared into the kitchen. A woman less dedicated to the challenge would have left by now. But Tia let the music wiggle her hips and shoulders and turn her for a look around the room. She found it neutral, simple, immaculate.

As Tia finished her turn, Sage appeared at her left side. She leaned close enough for the edge of her collar, falling open from the top two buttons, to graze the smooth bare skin of Tia's shoulder. Close enough to allow her cologne to linger, to bring her lips close to Tia's ear.

"You've made this much too easy," Sage whispered.

Tia laughed, the spontaneous laugh of one high roller acknowledging another, and offered Sage her drink.

Sage tasted it over Tia's shoulder, but didn't take the glass. "Keep it," she said in a saucy tone. "I won't disturb it."

At that, she knelt on one knee, and carefully lifted the edge of the dress at the bottom of the slit. Exposé beat out their warning, "I think I'm in trouble." The warning wasn't meant for Sage. At a pace half that of the music, she painstakingly lifted the material away from the long leg until she reached the top of the opening. There it hugged snuggly over the long muscle of Tia's thigh.

She controlled the urge to look up. Whatever expression was in Tia's eyes would be sacrificed for sliding the tip of the scissors so carefully under the edge of the slit that not even the cool of the steel would be felt. She lifted and slid and made the first cut.

The sound Tia uttered, not quite a moan but more than a sigh, told Sage what she wanted to know; she had not expected irreverence to this extent. She could feel the weight of Tia's eyes now, following the ruinous path of the scissors through the shimmer over her hip and the tightness of her waist to the bareness of her back. Then with two final snips the straps gave way, and in seconds the pricey original dropped and folded into a worthless heap on the floor.

Tia stared in disbelief at the top of Sage's head. It was all she could see now as Sage moved around her to snip away the last of her decency, a black thong.

Sage stood and circled her prize. No emotion registered in her eyes as they made their assessment of the woman, whom designers paid ten thousand dollars a day to dress, standing naked before her.

"You're inexcusably arrogant," Tia said, followed by the last swallow of her martini.

Sage said nothing. Her eyes remained on Tia's. She began unbuttoning her shirt at a pace she knew would stretch the fabric of Tia's composure. She looked for signs of anxiousness, desire—something, anything that indicated what she was feeling or thinking. But what she saw was an image of herself reflected back.

The sound filling the room beat like a synthesized heart, and Sade breathed over and over again a prophetic promise, "This is no ordinary love, no ordinary love."

Her shirt hung open, the zipper of her pants undone. Sage dropped her eyes to remove her pants, and in an instant found herself on her knees. With surprising strength Tia's hand pushed down against her shoulder, while the other hand grasped the hair of her head. The fabric had reached the tearing point.

Sage gripped a long thigh to regain her balance. Tia immediately widened her stance and forced Sage's head between her legs. There was no resistance. They had arrived at a place where power negated power. No one would win because no one would lose. Satisfaction was what mattered now, and pleasure. What did youth know of courtship or relationships or commitment? What concerns did it have? What thoughts of tomorrow?

Sliding her hands up the lean length of Tia's legs, Sage grasped the small buttocks and felt Tia shiver in anticipation. She was forced to override the inclination to tease with her lips the narrow patch of hair, to brush them delicately around the edges.

Instead, she pressed her mouth fully up into the moist heat and found quickly what tightened Tia's grip and commanded an involuntary gasp of excitement.

Tia would tolerate no teasing, no more waiting, and Sage would accommodate her. If mental foreplay was all that she needed, then it was all she would get. If a fast track to orgasm was what she wanted, then Sage would take her there as hard and as fast as she could. A short fuse burns quickly.

They did only what was necessary, nothing more. Tia

rubbing and pressing and somehow remaining balanced on two-inch heels. Sage stroking and thrusting with her tongue until wetness ran a stream from her jaw, down the curve of her throat, and trickled between her breasts.

The lyrics kept their cadence, "This is no . . ." Tia shouted with the thrust that sent her into orgasm. "No ordinary love . . . " Her fingers, twisted into Sage's hair, pulled with ferocity. Sage pressed up hard and finished as deep inside as she could. "No ordinary love."

The thought that that might be it, that their game of challenge would end there with one burst of orgasm, was as short-lived as the fuse that had led to it. It was only the beginning of something neither of them had really ever defined.

There would be many more nights devoted to pleasure—spontaneous meetings, impulsive sex, and a trail of public displays of pomp and splendor. Who caught who would never be answered, nor did it need to be. They served each other quite well.

"I know you, Sage Bristo," Tia was saying, undraping herself from Sage's shoulders and circling behind her. "We're more alike than not."

"You know only what you see," Sage replied.

"I know what those lips have done to me so many times, what pleasure these hands have in store." She touched her fingertips lightly down the length of Sage's arm and slipped her palm under her hand. "How you love to make me wait."

"We've had this conversation, Tia."

"Yes," she said, stepping directly in front of Sage. "Must we have it every time? Can't we dispense with such trivialities?"

As she looked into Tia's eyes, all these years later, she wondered if what she saw there was still herself reflected back. "Love isn't trivial."

Tia began unfastening the buttons of her blouse. "It's a messy emotion," she said, unfastening the last two buttons and dropping the blouse from her shoulders, "that destroys good relationships."

Chapter 28

Deanne was startled awake by something cold and wet touching her lips. She took a sharp breath and blinked back at the aqua eyes staring at her from the edge of the night-stand. Seconds later, she realized that she had fallen asleep, finally, in the early hours of the morning, on Sage's side of the bed.

The phone still lay next to the pillow, but it hadn't rung all night. She lifted her head from the pillow still damp from her tears.

"Come here, sweetie. Come on," she said, lifting the kitten onto the bed. "I can't see the clock." When she could, it showed the hour was late enough not to be rude. She dialed Cimmie's number.

For three anxious rings, she agonized about what she would say. *Why didn't you call? Where were you?* Or she would ask no questions at all. She would gladly have endured a night of worry and tears for nothing, if only Sage had fallen asleep and forgotten.

"Cim? I hope I'm not calling too early. How are you feeling?"

"A few sharp twinges now and then, and a horrendous backache. I think she's doing gymnastics in here. Jeff's just starting breakfast. He liked those pancakes we made when you were here so well that he wants to try to make them himself."

"Oh, so he wasn't just being polite. I haven't tried them out on Sage yet."

There was an unusually awkward silence in place of Cimmie's automatic offer to put Sage on the phone.

The marbles started dropping to the bottom of Deanne's stomach. She wanted Cimmie to say something without having to ask the question, but she didn't. Deanne cleared her throat. "Sage said she'd call last night. I guess she forgot. Could you put her on the phone, Cim?"

"I'll have to have her call you back, Dee."

The last marble shattered the pile in the pit of her stomach. "She's not there, is she?"

"She—"

"Was she gone all night?" *Sequins and tails.* "Was she with Tia?"

After a slight hesitation, "Yes." Then quickly Cimmie added, "It was some political thing, a fund-raiser. It probably got late and she didn't want to wake us."

Tears were rolling down Deanne's cheeks, but anger kept her voice strong. "What do you really think?"

"I think she was inconsiderate and insensitive."

"And unfaithful."

"I didn't say that."

"You didn't have to. We both know her history with Tia." Deanne lay on her back, the tears wetting her hair and rolling into her free ear. Purrs were interrupted by little squeaks as the kitten licked at the wetness. Deanne pushed her away, but the kitten kept coming back.

"Dee, don't jump to a conclusion that may not be true. Sage was a little miffed at me last night when she left."

"Tia's been e-mailing her at work. I found out accidentally. If there's nothing to it, why hasn't she told me?" Cimmie apparently had no ready answer. "Did you know she was going to New York to go to this thing with Tia?"

"No. It made her mad when I questioned her reason for being here. Part of me feels horrible for doubting her."

"And the other part?"

"She *does* love you, Deanne. I know that for sure."

Sitting on the edge of the bed, tears still streaming down her face, Deanne tipped her head back and exhaled a painful sound. "I can't believe this is happening again in my life."

It was obvious now to Cimmie that she was crying. "Dee, you don't know that anything happened."

"No, I never do. I'm always the last to know."

Chapter 29

"Call Deanne," Cimmie commanded, the second Sage walked in the door.

She was dressed in tuxedo pants and shirt and carrying the jacket. "I tried already this morning. There was no answer."

"She knows about last night. She knows you were with Tia."

Sage tossed her jacket over the arm of the couch, and picked up the phone. With a long, audible exhale she dropped into the chair. She waited through ten or eleven rings before hanging up.

Cimmie returned to the living room with a glass of orange juice and handed it to Sage. "Did you get her?"

Shaking her head, she said, "No. And she turned off the answering machine. Here, sit down," she directed. "You shouldn't be waiting on anyone."

"Don't make me sit. My back is hurting again. Walking is

more comfortable, really." She headed back toward the kitchen with Sage following. "You're as bad as Jeff."

"What?" Jeff asked, placing a plate on the table.

"Nothing," Cimmie replied. "After Sage eats and changes clothes, I want you two to pick up some things for me. I'll make out a list so you won't have to remember it all."

"I knew somehow we would end up shopping together," Sage grumbled, placing a gallon of milk in the cart.

"Actually, I don't mind shopping."

"Then you're a better wife than I am. What else is left on the list?"

"Baby stuff. The other side of the store."

Sage followed him down the aisles as he navigated stacks of unshelved stock, loose children, oblivious women and their unattended carts, all things that would push her past her patience level after the first aisle.

He stopped amid shelves of formula and diapers and turned to face Sage. "You know, I'm not trying to be the better spouse."

"Aren't you?"

"No," he protested. "I'm not competing with you."

"Okay," she said, snatching the list from his hand.

"Wait a minute, Sage. You think I *am.*"

Sage looked up from the list. "Yeah." So matter-of-fact was her response that it obviously surprised Jeff. She jumped on her advantage. "How carefully you charted Cimmie's cycles, watched her nutrition. How understanding you are of the most dysfunctional family in the universe, of me. The perfect negotiator quells the fears, secures the eggs. The perfect mate. You haven't missed a chance to let me know that."

"I only wanted you to know that I was taking good care of her. Maybe you really can't accept that a straight man can be nurturing and sensitive to a woman's needs."

She tossed a package of pacifiers into the cart and returned immediately to the eyes still fixed on her. "Or maybe *you* don't accept that I *can*. After all I am a dyke. Everyone knows how dykes feel about men."

"I'm sorry, I didn't realize that you felt this way."

"I'm not good with pretense—projecting or accepting."

"You think I've been pretentious."

"Can you tell me you don't believe that a child would be better raised by you and Cimmie? That you never assumed that a lesbian relationship, especially mine, was too unstable, too destined for breakup to attempt raising a child? And now, when Deanne and I are having obvious problems, haven't you secretly justified that and said 'See, they're not going to make it'?"

She held his bewildered stare for a moment, then scooped a box of newborn diapers off the shelf and stooped to slide it under the cart. She hesitated, still in a stoop, as if she had a catch in her back and couldn't straighten. Then, very slowly, she stood. Her gaze seemed distant, her eyes not registering on anything specific.

"We'll get the rest of the things later," she said hurriedly. "Come on, we have to go."

"Now what, Sage?" he said with an exasperated frown.

"She kicked us out of there because we were hovering over her like two mother hens."

But he was talking to her back. Sage had reached full stride and was about to leave him standing alone in the middle of the aisle.

"Cim?" Sage called, entering the apartment ahead of Jeff and dropping a bag of groceries on the coffee table.

"In here, Sage," Cimmie called from the bedroom.

"Are you all right?"

"Funny you should ask," she said with a faint attempt at a smile. She was semi-sitting on the edge of the bed, propped up by pillows that were stacked against the headboard. "My water broke just after you left. And," she added, picking up the cellular phone beside her, "neither of you remembered this."

Sage rushed to her and took her arm. Jeff was right behind her. They stumbled over each other's sentences. "I knew we shouldn't have—"

"How far apart—"

"Relax," Cimmie said, gently pulling her arms free. "Both of you stop and take a breath. The contractions haven't started yet, and the Lamaze instructor said not to panic. We have up to eighteen hours before anyone starts getting worried. That's a long time." She grimaced as she moved to sit up straighter. "I am glad you're back, though."

Jeff sat on the bed next to her and took her hand. "But this is way early."

"I have a call in to the doctor. She's in delivery right now,

174

but the nurse will notify her. She told me to get my things together while I'm waiting and not to worry. We have a while yet."

"What do you need us to do?" Sage asked.

"I got my bag out over there, but my back started hurting again, so it isn't packed yet. Jeff can pack it. Maybe you could get my toiletries together. There's a little maroon-colored—ahhhh," she exclaimed, closing her eyes and clenching her fists in obvious pain.

Jeff turned from the closet. "What?"

Cimmie's face was tense with pain. "Ohhh. *This*"—she forced the words tightly through a held breath—"has to be a contraction."

"We can get these things later," Sage said. "Let's get you to the car."

As the pain subsided, Cimmie reassured her. "This is just the beginning of the fun. Now we get to see how well we paid attention in our Lamaze class."

"If we go in too early, they'll only send us home to wait," Jeff explained. "They don't want to see us until the contractions are about five minutes apart."

Suddenly, Cimmie cried out in pain. Jeff immediately checked his watch.

"This can't be right," he said. "It hasn't been much more than five minutes, and we're just beginning labor."

"Oh god," Cimmie exclaimed, rocking from side to side against the pillows. Beads of perspiration glistened above her top lip.

Sage stroked her head. "What can I do?"

Cimmie shook her head and closed her eyes, and continued to rock. Then finally she was still, and her body sank again into the pillows. "Oh god, if this is only the beginning pains, I'm not going to make it through the big ones."

Jeff reclaimed her hand and kissed it. "You're going to do just fine."

"*You,*" she said with a glare, "have *no* idea."

Not quite five minutes later, Cimmie was once more wrenching in pain. Concerned that the contractions were too close too early, Jeff called the hospital. He was reassured that they would most likely become more erratic, not only in pattern, but in intensity, and that there was nothing to worry about. He concentrated on packing, and Sage took over the timing.

Over the next hour, the contractions varied as the nurse had predicted. Sage and Jeff took turns trying to keep Cimmie's mind off the pain, wiping her face and neck with a cool cloth, talking comfortingly about how the Lamaze instructor had told them it would happen.

"I don't know how to describe it to you," Cimmie said during a period of relief. "It's like the swelling pain you feel building before you explode with diarrhea, but, it's much more intense and you don't explode."

Then shortly after that, the signs became unmistakable— fierce contractions every four or five minutes, Cimmie shouting in pain that her skin was on fire. And the words none of them were prepared for:

"Oh no. I have to push," Cimmie gasped.

Startled, Jeff grabbed for the phone and instructed her, "No. Try not to push. You can't push yet." His hands were trembling as he tried to dial.

Cimmie was crying. "I can't stop it. I can't stop."

And Sage was stripping off Cimmie's clothes.

"Forget the hospital, Jeff," she ordered. "Call nine-one-one." She turned to face him so that Cimmie couldn't hear her. "And if they don't hurry, I think we're going to be delivering this baby ourselves."

His voice shook as he spoke to the operator. But with the phone at his ear, he swiftly followed orders, gathering what may be needed, reassuring Cimmie as she rested.

He met the seriousness in Sage's eyes. "She'll stay on the phone with us as long as we need her. The emergency squad is on the way."

They had only hurriedly prepared the bed when Cimmie was gripped again by contractions. "Ahhh, no. Here we go. I can't stop it."

"It's okay, honey," Jeff said, poised on the end of the bed. "We're ready. It's okay. Push all you can."

Her hand caught in Cimmie's deathlike grip, Sage asked, "Can I touch you now? Can I hold you?"

"I don't care," she blurted. "I don't care. I can't stand this. I can't do it."

Sage helped her lean forward into her push, and slid behind her. She wrapped her arms around her and let Cimmie grasp both hands. Sage held her as she pushed and shouted, and watched as Jeff conversed with the operator and waited.

"You're doing great, honey," he said calmly. "Breathe now like they told you. Don't hold your breath . . . that's good, baby. That's good."

"Let me take the pain, Cim. Breathe in the strength from my arms, blow the pain out to me . . . Let me take it. That's it," Sage whispered, as Cimmie collapsed against her. "I'll always take it."

Long, wet curls clung stubbornly around Cimmie's neck and face. Sage pressed her face to the damp head and felt Cimmie's body beginning to tense again. "Breathe in the strength," Sage said softly. "You're incredible, Cimmie. So incredibly strong. Breathe it in and force out the pain."

Her voice had more strength this time, more conviction. "Ohh, here we go. Here we go . . . oh god." Sage helped her lean into her strongest effort yet. It erupted into a sound like a weightlifter muscling a massive burden.

Jeff, with the phone pressed in place against his ear by his shoulder, stroked the calves of Cimmie's legs. He spoke into the phone as calmly as he could. "I can see the baby's head." He listened to instructions, then, "Okay, honey, you have to push again now, just like the last one. Push with all you have." His hands shook as he straightened the towel for the baby.

"One more, Cim," Sage said softly. "She's on her way. You'll be able to hold her in your arms." She leaned forward against Cimmie's weight. "Come on now, with everything you have."

"Okay," Cimmie gasped. "Okay." She bore down hard, squeezing Sage's hands so tightly that the fingers turned purple. The sound she rendered was one of anguish, and a powerful need to finish.

The excitement in Jeff's voice was apparent. "She's coming." And full of wonder. "Oh my god . . . " And touchingly tender. "Oh my god, Cimmie."

Cimmie collapsed in a cry of relief. Sage wiped long, dark strands of hair from Cimmie's cheek and kissed her face. "I am so proud of you. I love you, Cim."

Weakly Cimmie asked, "Is she okay? Can I see her?"

"She's perfect," Jeff replied.

Sage propped the pillows back under Cimmie's head as Jeff rose and placed his treasure, shaking and crying and wrapped in a towel, on Cimmie's chest.

Tears flowed freely down his cheeks as he said, "I have never seen anything so incredible." He leaned and held Cimmie's face in his hands. "Are you all right?"

"I am now," she said, closing her eyes. She reached out her hand on the other side of the bed for Sage.

Sage took it and sat next to her. The baby had quieted. She was blue and white and blotchy, but at that moment, she was the most beautiful thing on this earth. Sage touched her fingertips carefully over the tiny face. Tears filled her eyes.

"*Qua, my ne-wa-ah' na-o'-geh*," she said quietly. "*Go-ah'-wuk* of the Doe.

Chapter 30

Not answering the phone works very well for avoiding someone you don't want to talk to or for avoiding a decision you're not really ready to make. But it is almost a surefire way to miss important emergency messages.

Luckily there are friends like Kasey, who will take a phone call from New York late on a Sunday night and deliver the message to the door personally.

Deanne booked the first available flight, called Jeff, and when she arrived at Cimmie's door had still not spoken to Sage. When the door opened and she had her first chance, she said only what was necessary.

"Deanne—"

"Don't say anything, Sage."

"Let me—"

"No," she said, holding her hand up and shaking her head. "If I trust you, there should be no questions asked. If I don't, nothing you say is going to make any difference."

She had already crossed the living room. "I need to see Cimmie and the baby, then I need some time alone."

Sage stood just inside the bedroom door. Deanne kissed and embraced Jeff and then Cimmie, then held in her arms the miracle. Part of Jeff, part of Sage, a creation so unique that it was like no other in the history of the world. *That,* she realized, was the miracle of it—not the order of birth, as difficult to affect as it had been, but the uniqueness of this new being. Such a huge conception for something so tiny and innocent.

"A miracle," she said, kissing the warm, velvety head. "You're a miracle." *How many times have I dismissed that word as merely overstated joy.* "Oh, Cimmie, she's beautiful."

Cimmie smiled, wide and relaxed. A pinkish glow radiated from her face. "She has beautiful parents."

The baby stirred awake in Deanne's arms. Her eyelids opened only briefly, then closed to cover eyes still sensitive to even the dim light of the bedroom. Little arms jerked upward, fingers opening and closing, until the baby's hand rested against Deanne's chest. The tiny fingers gripped the cloth of her sweater, and she turned her head to nuzzle a guppylike mouth to Deanne's breast.

"Oops, I think she wants something I can't give her." She carefully placed the baby back in Cimmie's lap.

"She's showing off the second best thing she does." Cimmie lifted the edge of her sweatshirt and cradled the baby against her breast.

"I'll leave her to eat in peace," Deanne said quietly. "I still have some things to think over. I'm going to walk down to the coffee shop."

Cimmie nodded. "Jeff, honey, will you go with her?"

"Sure. Come on, Dee."

Deanne shook her head. "Thanks, Jeff, but I have some serious thinking to do."

Sage took hold of her arm as she passed. "Let Jeff go with you. It's not safe."

She met Sage's eyes straight on. "Not letting me think this through is much more dangerous."

It was probably ridiculous to expect an hour or so in a coffee shop to do much toward giving her direction or settling her mind. But there had been no dreams that she could remember, and no advice that anyone had given her that made making a decision any easier.

Ironically, she wasn't sure what it was she was deciding. *Whether or not I trust Sage? Or whether I will be able to forgive her? Maybe both. If there's trust, there's no need to forgive. If there isn't . . .*

The elevator was empty and Deanne was deep in thought when it sighed to rest on the lobby floor of the apartment building. The start she felt when the doors opened rivaled the discovery of a large spider crawling across your pillow. She quickly tried to compose herself and stepped from the elevator.

Before the woman, now beside her, could step in, Deanne surprised herself at what came out of her own mouth. "Excuse me," she heard herself say. "Are you Tia?"

"Yes," she replied. Perfect teeth glistened brilliantly white within a glossy, plum smile. "I haven't modeled in years." She busily retrieved a piece of paper from her purse and scribbled her name on it. "It's nice to know people still recognize me," she said, handing the autograph to Deanne.

Hesitating only briefly, Deanne produced her own pen, turned the paper over, signed her own name and returned it to a surprised Tia. "Maybe you've read one of my books."

Tia recovered quickly. "I have," she admitted, while her eyes took in the whole of Deanne's face. "I apologize for not recognizing *you*."

"No need. I don't expect two books to make Demore a household name."

Tia's eyes dropped, then a second later rose with a tilt of her head. "I was on my way up to see Cimmie and the baby—"

"And Sage."

The plum lips pursed before widening into a close-lipped smile.

When you can't cover the spider with a Kleenex and wad it into instant death, you carefully inch away to a more acceptable distance.

But before Deanne could move, Tia set out her bait. "Would you like to go somewhere and have coffee with me?"

"Yes, I would," she heard herself say.

"I enjoyed your book very much," Tia began. "If there is such a thing as hysterical truth, you've mastered it."

They sat amid the clinks and late-night chatter of the coffee shop, with only the distance of a small round table between them.

"You may enjoy the next book even more."

Tia acknowledged the arrival of their coffee with a nod and reached for the little container of nondairy creamer. "I'll be sure to look for it," she said, somehow opening the creamer with long plum-colored nails that had no purpose beyond modeling that Deanne could think of. "What is it called?"

"*The Women of the Doe.*" Deanne sipped cautiously and waited for Tia's eyes. *Where the hell are you going with this?* "You may see a part of Sage Bristo that you didn't know was there." *Oh, what are you saying?*

Confident eyes left the uncertainty of Deanne's to watch fingers bedazzled with gold and gems swirl the creamer to a dusky tan. "I love this color. A perfect skin color, don't you think? Luscious."

The reference was understood and ignored.

"I could write a book of my own about Sage Bristo," Tia continued.

"I suppose you could."

"I could call it *Sequins and Tails*. Or *T-a-l-e-s. Tales.*" She smiled in self-amusement. "But I don't kiss and tell."

"No. I suppose not." *How close can I get before my feet get caught in the web, and the spider has me right where she wants me?* "Nor does Sage, easily."

"What *has* she told you about me?"

Careful. "That you were friends and lovers for years before I met her. That you maintain a mutually needed friendship."

"Then you know that she sees me every chance she gets."

Every time she's in New York? Every month? Are you ready to hear this? Deanne pulled her eyes from Tia's directness and concentrated on her cup. "Are you implying that there is more than a friendship between you?"

"I'm saying that sex means different things to different people. For some it can be a nice way of saying 'I've missed you' or 'Thank you' or 'Good-bye until I see you again.'" She sipped from her cup as if she had no idea that her words may have completely devastated Deanne's life. "Just another aspect of friendship," she added. "Are you okay with that?"

Deanne could feel the hairs on her arms raising under her sweater. "No. I'm not. That's not only asking me to contradict my belief in what commitment means, but to believe that Sage is lying to me."

"We spent the night together Saturday night."

She was caught, like a fly in a web, fluttering in fear. Heart pounding, Deanne stared into the face of intimidating beauty, the face of a challenge she had feared for four years. Suddenly the fluttering stopped. "I know." The fear was gone. "And I know that she didn't make love to you."

Deanne took a deep breath while the look on Tia's face changed slowly in the silence. Questioning formed in the soft fold above the bridge of her nose. There was disbelief in the turn of her lips.

I've either made myself the biggest fool in the universe or I know Sage Bristo better than she can believe.

Tia finally spoke. "Certainly not from my lack of trying, and I'm *very* good. Sage, though, is her own woman. She never surprises me—but you *do*. You trust her, don't you?"

Had she believed her own words? Or were they uttered only in defense against a woman giving her every reason not to believe them? *Yes.* In that instant when the fear left her and she had said the words out loud, she believed them. "She has never once lied to me. If I would trust her with my life, wouldn't I trust her with my heart?"

The web lay in a tangled mess. The spider dangled by one thin strand. "Well, don't deceive yourself for a moment that she wasn't tempted, because she was."

"I doubt there are many who wouldn't be. You're incredibly beautiful, Tia. I have no illusions of being able to compete with that at all. But love has its own beauty."

"So she says."

Deanne leaned forward, folded arms resting casually on the table's edge. The strand had been broken, the spider was falling. "Have you ever held her head against your breast with tears running down her face? Ever felt the trembling of the little girl inside her that got walled up so fast that she never knew childhood? Or heard her whispers of fear in the middle of the night?"

Tia's face questioned again, but this time her eyes seemed unfocused, as if to allow her thoughts better inward sight. Very slowly she shook her head.

"Love has the patience to do that. And the time to tend to

more than the physical. Love asks, 'What else do you need?' and isn't afraid of the answer. And when lust has been satisfied and walks away, love's right there with its arms around you."

"Spoken like a writer."

"Spoken in friendship, if you want it."

Tia stared for a moment. Finally she admitted, "I had other intentions."

"Yes, I know."

"You're taking very good care of my friend, aren't you?"

"We're trying to take good care of each other."

"I never thought I'd ever say this, especially to you," Tia said, her brow knit with sincerity. "I think if Sage had ever felt for me what she feels for you, I would have destroyed it long ago."

"Sage, stop pacing and sit down," Cimmie directed. You're making me nervous."

"It's too dangerous wandering around alone. She's so stubborn," she said, dropping into the chair at the end of the bed. "She makes me crazy."

"What makes you crazy is that she's as strong-willed as you are. Face it," she said with a loving smile, "you've met your match."

"I'm giving her fifteen more minutes, then I'm going after her. I don't care how mad it makes her."

"Relax," Jeff said, laying his jacket on the end of the bed. "I just checked the coffee shop. She's talking with who I'm guessing could be Tia."

Sage groaned and laid her head back on the back of the chair.

Cimmie laughed. "I hope you don't have any secrets, big sister."

"I'm sure I don't any more. Tia's not one to let a chance like this slip by."

"It helps if you have nothing to hide."

"I don't, really," Sage contended. "But I can't expect that she'll believe I was thinking only of her love with Tia in my arms—naked."

"Ohhh, *good*," Cimmie chided. "My sister the nun."

Jeff held his finger to his lips as Deanne peered in through the bedroom door, then waved her in.

Cimmie and the baby were asleep on the bed next to him. Sage was asleep in the chair. Deanne stopped beside the bed.

Jeff whispered. "Is everything okay?"

"Yes," she whispered back. "It is. I'll get Sage out of here so you can get some sleep. We'll see you in the morning."

Deanne leaned over Sage, took the hand draped over the arm of the chair, and whispered, "Come on, honey. Come to bed."

Sage rose without a word and followed her into the guest room.

"Before you say anything," Deanne began. "I have something to tell you." She held her hand over her heart. "I had to know if I believed in here that you've been faithful to me. I thought that I'd get the answer from Tia." She shook her head. "But I realized that I already knew the answer without her telling me."

Sage grabbed Deanne into her arms and held her tightly. "I haven't loved anyone like I do you. I don't want to do anything to lose you."

Deanne pressed her hands over Sage's back and laid her head against her shoulder. "I know that now."

"I know I can't make a family without you. It takes more than blood."

"That's what I needed to hear. It means more to me than anything you could say right now."

"It all makes perfect sense now." Sage was stroking her fingers through the back of Deanne's hair, her cheek resting against her forehead. "I didn't understand how important it was to you, I guess because you already had such a close family. I never realized how much you needed one with me."

They were nose to nose now, standing in the darkness, only beginning to feel the relief from the bands of tension that had tightened around their days and nights for months.

But for Sage it was as if the long-suffering pain of a toothache had suddenly stopped. Relieved on the surface, while her subconscious remained ready for its return.

Deanne took a long, deep breath and closed her eyes. She exhaled and opened them to a welcomed smile. "I feel like I just took the first fresh breath of spring. The one that you take in so deeply that your lungs stop at their fullest and don't want to give it up."

"I haven't even said it yet."

"Said what?"

"That I haven't slept with Tia, or anyone else, since before you even admitted that you were in love with me."

"I tried to tell you," Deanne said softly, "you don't have to say it." She began placing kisses on the warm skin under Sage's collar.

"I've wanted only you from the first night I saw you; when I smiled at you and you blushed," Sage said, nuzzling her lips into Deanne's hair. "I was sure Sharon would embarrass you, and you'd never come back to play cards again."

Deanne lifted her face to the attention of Sage's lips, touching lightly over her eyelids and her cheeks. "You can still make me blush."

"I know." Her hands gently raised the bottom of Deanne's sweater. "You blush whenever I first touch you to let you know that I want to make love to you . . . like now."

The sweater slipped easily over her head. Sage's hands, cool on the warming skin, slid under the back of Deanne's sports bra and moved expertly to the sides and up to remove it.

"You're so warm."

Deanne whispered, "For you."

The sensation of aroused, naked skin brushed by cool, crisp cotton was an eroticism Sage was well aware of. She remained fully clothed as she disrobed Deanne, lacing her only in kisses, and holding her against her.

The instant her loins touched against the denim of Sage's jeans, Deanne knew that it was her gratification, and only hers, that Sage intended. Unselfish lips would be slow and patient and ardent and fierce. Knowing hands would make her want and paint her flush.

Satisfying thoughts of family and faithful love were quickly replaced with murmurs and secret places and no thoughts at all. The night became a tangle of sheets and limbs, emotions dancing free, and desire racing toward fulfillment.

Without clouds of worry to interfere, their hearts, open to pleasure and pleasing, soared. The hours were filled with love and promises and plans, until early into the morning.

Finally they slept. Deanne cradled peacefully against Sage's shoulder, until suddenly Sage bolted upright in the darkness.

"Wha—"

Sage quickly covered Deanne with her body and pinned her to the bed. "Shhh," she warned in a whisper.

Deanne waited under the tension of Sage's body, trying to gain her own bearings. Carefully she asked, "What is it?"

Still in a whisper, Sage replied, "Didn't you hear it?"

"I didn't hear anything."

"It was a gunshot."

Deanne listened carefully for a moment, then worked an arm free and stretched it across Sage's back. "There was nothing, honey," she said in a soft whisper. "It was only a dream. Everything is okay."

Sage raised up slightly and listened intently. The baby fussed briefly in the other bedroom, then quieted.

Softly Deanne reassured her, "It's okay, honey. Try to relax."

Sage released a long sigh. Her body softened and collapsed around Deanne. "It sounded so real."

"It was just a bad dream. Do you remember any of it?"

She shook her head, her heart still racing. "I'm sorry I woke you," she said as she lifted and slipped from the bed. "I'll get us something to drink."

Deanne watched her don a pair of underwear and a shirt and leave for the kitchen. A trip she knew would include a thorough inspection of the apartment.

Chapter 31

Sage stepped from the shower to the sound of the hair dryer. She rubbed the large green towel over her head until she felt the blowing heat surround her feet and begin working its way up her legs. She peered from beneath the towel to be greeted with a bright Demore smile and a kiss.

"Turn around," Deanne said. "I'll dry your back."

She finished toweling her hair while the heat quickly warmed her damp skin. Deanne circled and dried as much of her as Sage would allow, then turned off the dryer. "Too hot on the front?"

"You get a little too close," Sage replied. "But thank you."

"I'm so excited," Deanne started, tucking the bottom of her navy pullover into her jeans. "Can you believe Jeff is going to take the position at Eastern?"

"I think I'll reserve excitement until after they actually move. But Cimmie seems sure that her bank will transfer her to a branch in Ann Arbor."

Deanne grabbed her in a joyful hug before Sage could fasten her pants. "They're going to be so close. Could you ever have imagined it would be this way? You'll be a part of her life. We'll be able to watch her grow up."

Sage offered a sincere smile. "A whole lot fewer trips to New York."

Deanne planted a quick kiss on Sage's cheek and handed her the hair dryer. "Hurry and dry your hair, and let's go see the baby." She beamed happily.

The knock on the bedroom door was so soft that Deanne nearly dismissed it as something else. Jeff's face, when the door opened, held an expression that caught her breath short.

"What's wrong? Is the baby okay?"

His voice was barely more than a whisper. "The baby's fine," he said, but added solemnly, "Sage's father is here. It might be wise for you two to stay in the bedroom until he leaves."

"Does he know Sage is here?"

"I don't know. But Cimmie's not going to tell him."

"Okay," she said, looking toward the bathroom. "I'm a little nervous, though, about how Sage will react."

"She'll be all right," he assured her. "She doesn't want an uncomfortable situation any more than we do."

"Is Lena with him?"

"No. It's just John. We'll try to keep his visit short."

"Thanks," she said with a squeeze of his hand.

"Jeff was wonderful," Cimmie was saying. "I didn't know that the back pains I was having were early labor pains. When we realized how far along I was, it was too late to get to the hospital."

John Capra extended his hand to Jeff as he entered the living room. "Not an easy thing for a man to do."

Jeff shrugged modestly. "I had a lot of help. The, uh, nine-one-one operator kept me from falling apart. The emergency team arrived in time to cut the umbilical cord."

The two men moved to join Cimmie on the other side of the room. She stood and the baby stirred awake in her arms. A little arm jerked free of the blanket, and fingers grasped at empty air. John offered a long index finger for the tiny hand to grab hold of.

"Not much of a grip yet," he said, lifting the corners of his mouth into what nearly resembled a smile. "Will she have your nose, Cimmie?"

"I think she was lucky and inherited Jeff's." She flashed a look at Jeff that warned him that she was in turmoil.

He offered a diversion. "John, can I get you a cup of coffee?"

"Yes, that would be fine."

Alone with his daughter, John opened his hands and gestured toward the baby. "May I?" he asked with another attempt at a smile.

Cimmie's thoughts, conflicting and disguised in emotion, pushed and shoved for control. *If the baby starts crying . . . Had he been tender with them as babies? What reason would he have to hurt her?*

She kissed the velvety soft head. He gestured again. *The beginning of reconciliation.* Carefully she placed the peach-and-green clad bundle in his hands.

It was a nervous smile that greeted Jeff's return. "A good time for Grandpa to meet his granddaughter," she explained, "while she's sweet smelling and sleepy." *Ballistic* was the only word that came to mind. *Sage would be ballistic if she knew.*

Sage paced the small bedroom like a caged tigress. She stopped only long enough to load her gun and place it on the bed.

Deanne strained the very limit of a whisper. "What are you doing?"

"I don't know," she admitted. "I don't want any surprises."

"That's crazy, Sage. Put it away."

Sage turned abruptly and pointed at the gun. "It stays where it is."

"Why didn't Mom come with you?" Cimmie asked, watching her father's every movement.

He cradled the baby against his brown wool blazer and gazed into her face. It was a sight Cimmie had never imagined she would see. "I have other business as well today."

"You could have left her here to visit and picked her up later. That would have been fine."

"She'll come another time." Then, in the same casual tone of voice, he asked, "Is Celia here?"

His composure didn't fool her. It felt as though her heart would beat itself to death. She wanted to run, to find someplace safe, where she couldn't hear the thunder or see the lightning strike. She breathed in deeply and focused on the innocence he held in his arms. She managed a reply she knew should not have been delayed even a second. "She was here yesterday."

"You were never very good at lying, were you?"

"Here, John," Jeff interjected. "I'll trade you a cup of coffee for a baby." He smiled and offered the cup. "She's probably ready for a diaper change."

John made no effort toward the exchange. Instead he moved slowly back to the front of the room. "Tell Celia I'd like to talk to her."

Jeff persisted calmly, "Why don't we just visit, John. There are a lot of things I've wanted to talk with you about, man to man."

"Another time, Jeff." His focus found the hallway, where he directed his voice. "Celia!"

Sage turned toward the bedroom door and listened. The voice boomed again. "Celia!"

She snatched the gun from the bed and tucked it in the waistband behind her back.

Frightened, Deanne took her arm. "Don't, Sage," she whispered loudly. "Don't go out there."

"He knows I'm here. I don't want him coming in here after me." She started for the door and stopped. "You *have* to stay in here. If he sees you with me, he'll be all the more angry. Understand?"

When Sage emerged from the hallway, the air in the room hung with a stillness that bristled the hair on the back of her neck. The baby's quivering cries sounded in the distance, alone, unreachable.

Sage continued steadily toward her father. "You frightened the baby when you shouted. Let me give her to Jeff."

John's next move seemed to be an innocent shifting of the baby to one arm. But with no other warning, Sage was facing the barrel of a handgun pointing out from below the baby's blanket.

Sage stood pillar-still.

"Oh no," Cimmie gasped. "What have I done?"

"Whose baby is it?" John asked.

"It's Jeff and Cimmie's," she answered calmly. The baby continued to cry. "Look how frightened she is. Why don't you give her to her father?"

"Lena told me the fertility drugs didn't work." His eyes were direct, knowing. "Cimmie's eggs were bad."

"Her eggs only needed nourishment. Lena didn't know everything. Give Cimmie her baby now. Look how worried you've made her." She motioned carefully for Jeff to step forward. "You don't want to hurt the baby, not even accidentally. Let Jeff take her."

Jeff moved cautiously. When he was within reach of the baby, he said, "John, I'll take her and quiet her down."

John's attention, momentarily diverted, came abruptly back to Sage.

"It's me," Sage nodded. "It's me you want, John, not the

baby." Jeff's hands were around the baby, but she was still held firmly in John's grasp. Sage's eyes never left the center of the storm that was about to break. "I'll go with you. Just let go of her."

"I've got her, John. You can let go."

Finally, the release they'd been holding their breath for put the bundle safely in Jeff's hands. He backed away quickly and sent Cimmie and the baby out of the room.

She joined Deanne against the hallway wall where she had been watching and listening in horror. "Where's the phone?" Deanne whispered anxiously. "I can't find the phone."

Cimmie motioned in the direction of the kitchen, which was beyond the living room. "I think the cellular is still in Jeff's briefcase." She peered around the corner enough to see that the briefcase was still sitting in its usual place. "It's next to the door, right behind my father."

"Open the door, Mr. Capra," Sage directed, the gun still pointed squarely at her chest, "so we can take our discussion out into the hall."

His stare was relentless, hers unflinching. He opened the door and motioned with the gun for her to leave first. When she was directly opposite him, she turned so that she faced him as she backed out the door.

"Close it, Jeff," she instructed. "And don't open it again unless I tell you to."

Deanne rushed from the hallway to the closed door.

"No," Jeff said, catching her by the shoulders. "It's too dangerous."

Cimmie ripped open the briefcase and grabbed the phone. Though her voice shook uncontrollably, she managed the essential information.

"We have to do something," Deanne pleaded.

"There's nothing more we can do." He scanned what he could see of the hallway through the door viewer. "He stepped away from the door. There's no way I could surprise him."

She appealed to Cimmie. "Would he really shoot her?"

Cimmie pulled her into a mutual embrace. She said nothing, but her body was shaking.

"No, please," she cried as fear began punching the air from her lungs. "I can't lose her." *Not now. Not like NaNan. Not when everything is finally right.* But the story was frighteningly clear now. The seed had been born, the legacy passed. Sage had done her job.

The gun was held steady. The gun hand supported it like a marksman. But the eyes sighting down its barrel were vacillating with desperation.

"Where's that insolent arrogance now?" he asked. "That disgusting irreverence for what is good and right?"

"Would you sacrifice the rest of your life on the likes of me?" Sage asked. "A woman? A lesbian? Is it worth your life?" *Of course it is. The perfect sacrifice for martyrdom. You're no man of idle threat. It didn't take a lifetime for me to know that.*

She thought about the gun in her waistband. Thought out the move it would take to get it precisely in her hand, her finger on the trigger. And the one it would take to drop and fire fast enough to avoid being shot. Possible—if his eyes wavered even once.

His eyes narrowed in gratification. "Would you feel *less* fear if you knew? More? If I do it too quickly, your stomach acid won't have time to churn and wrench its way up to your throat. You won't have time to realize the price you're going to pay for being an abomination on our society."

She ignored the words, watched his eyes, waited for his slightest lapse. Waited for her chance.

"But of course, I'll have to do it before the police arrive," he continued. "Because Jeff called them, out of his ignorance. So how much time do you have to live? Two more minutes? Three more minutes?"

She concentrated, went through the move to her gun in her mind. All the way through. Once. Twice. Focus direct on center. Watching the eye of the storm.

Then she saw it—a twitch in the cheek muscle below the left eye. There would be no more time to go through it again. Only the first second of the move. She could see it. She could feel the gun in her hand. *Steady your breath. Steady your hand. See it.*

Suddenly his eyes darted to the left, and Sage's gun was in her hand and she was dropping to her hip, and a shot rang out.

At the sound of the shot, Deanne pushed past Jeff and bolted out the door. John Capra lay in a contorted heap. Ten feet away, Sage sat on the floor, gun resting in her lap.

Standing beside her, gun still pointed at the crumpled, wounded man on the floor, was Lena Capra.

She mumbled the words in an unemotional daze, "It had to stop."

Sage rose in disbelief. She stood looking at the mother she had despised since childhood, and in that instant she saw the daughter NaNan thought she had lost.

Behind the tears welling in Lena's eyes was a strength Sage had never seen there before. Gone was the submissiveness in her voice. "I loved him once. He was a good man then."

She straightened her shoulders and turned to look into Sage's face. "I've always loved you."

There was a commotion of rushing footsteps and shouting orders as the police swarmed the hallway. Deanne froze against the wall, tears streaming down her face, while Sage clutched her mother in a protective embrace.

Lena's tears turned to sobs, and muffled words against Sage's chest. "I thought it was too late."

Sage pressed her cheek to her mother's head. "No," she said and closed her eyes. "We'll start here."

Marianne K. Martin

Marianne K. Martin is the author of the best-selling novels *Under the Witness Tree, Mirrors, Never Ending, Dawn of the Dance, Love in the Balance, Legacy of Love,* and the upcoming *Dance in the Key of Love.* She has been a Lambda Literary Award finalist for both *Under the Witness Tree* and *Mirrors.*

Before becoming a full-time writer, Martin had been a public-school teacher, a high school basketball and softball coach, a collegiate field hockey coach, and a photojournalist.

She has always been active in athletics and has played and coached ASA fast-pitch softball for many years. She also enjoys building and remodeling, drawing, landscaping, and reading.

Marianne K. Martin lives in Michigan with her partner and their two dogs.

Bywater Books

UNDER THE WITNESS TREE
by Marianne K. Martin

"*Under the Witness Tree* is a multi-dimensional love story woven with rich themes of family and the search for roots. This is a novel of discovery that reaches into the deeply personal and well beyond—into our community and its emerging history. Marianne Martin achieves new heights with this lovingly researched and intelligent novel."

Katherine V. Forrest

An aunt she didn't know existed leaves Dhari Weston with a plantation she knows she doesn't want.

Dhari's life is complicated enough without an antebellum albatross around her neck. Complicated enough without the beautiful Erin Hughes and her passion for historical houses, without Nessie Tinker, whose family breathed the smoke of General Sherman's march and who knows the secrets hidden in the ancient walls—secrets that could pull Dhari into their sway and into Erin's arms.

But Dhari's complicated life already has a girlfriend she wants to commit to, a family who needs her to calm the chaos of her mother's turbulent moods and a job that takes the rest of her time.

The last thing she needs are Civil War secrets that won't lie easy and a woman with secrets of her own . . .

ISBN 1-932859-00-4 $12.95

Available at your local bookstore
or to order call toll-free 866-390-7426
or order online at www.bywaterbooks.com

Bywater Books

DAWN OF THE DANCE
by Marianne K. Martin

"Marianne Martin is a wonderful story teller and a graceful writer with a light, witty touch with language and a sensitivity to the emotions of people in love. There is a tenderness and brightness to her characterizations that make the personalities quite beguiling." Ann Bannon

Three women live out one passion . . .

When Moni Matteson fell for Paige Flemming she thought her lonely days had come to an end. Paige, the sleek athlete with the mysterious past, taught Moni what it felt like to want, and to need, and finally to love. She also taught Moni what it felt like to be left—a devastation that shook Moni to the core and one that she wants never to repeat.

At college, Moni concentrates on her studies, on her art, and on her small group of friends. Romance is a thing of the past. But then she meets Katherine Cunningham, a beautiful woman with a sexy British accent . . .

Dawn of the Dance is the prequel to the
Lambda Literary Award finalist *Mirrors*.

ISBN 1-932859-05-5 $12.95

Bywater Books

DANCE IN THE KEY OF LOVE
by Marianne K. Martin

Paige Flemming is on the run. From the police, from her history, and from love itself. After sixteen years looking over her shoulder, she realizes it's time to run again. But when she pauses in her headlong flight to catch her breath with old friends, she crashes straight into another ghost from her past. And this time, it's not one she can easily escape.

Marissa Langford is a woman living with the wreckage of her dreams. A dancer deprived of the dance by a tragic accident, she is struggling to rebuild her life when Paige's appearance rekindles bitter memories of what she has lost. For both women, their meeting asks more questions than either can readily answer.

As they struggle with the turbulent emotions each provokes in the other, the net is closing on Paige. But cops are human too, and the hunter who has Paige in his sights has his own harsh emotional lessons to learn.

As old secrets emerge from the darkness, this finely drawn cast of characters search deep inside themselves for the resources to battle their demons. Desire walks hand in hand with betrayal, love is held hostage by abuse and shadows threaten dreams every step of the way.

In this long-awaited sequel to the best-selling lesbian romance *Dawn of the Dance*, Lambda Literary Award finalist Marianne K. Martin reminds us that there's no foot-work fancy enough to dance out of the shadow of the past.

ISBN 1-932859-17-9 $13.95 Available in June 2006